THE WEARY OPTIMIST

SMYTHE &
HUDDERSFIELD
BOOKS

THE WEARY OPTIMIST
Bad Bosses, Bad Jobs, Bad Sex,
&
"The 36 Reasons to Be Glad You Don't Work in Human Resources"

A NOVEL
by
Dale Dauten

SMYTHE &
HUDDERSFIELD
BOOKS

The Weary Optimist. Copyright ©2013 by Dale Dauten.

SMYTHE & HUDDERSFIELD BOOKS
visit SmytheandHuddersfield.com
For information on rights, signed copies or author appearances, contact Dale Dauten at dale@dauten.com.

Cover and interior design: Chris Molé
Cover illustration: Ted Goff

ISBN: 978-0-9897061-0-0

For Trevor and Joel,
and for the love of the long shot

SIR RICHARD (Iain Glen): Do you enjoy these games in which the player must appear ridiculous?

VIOLET (Maggie Smith): Sir Richard, life is a game in which the player must appear ridiculous.

From *Downton Abbey*
by Julian Fellowes

. . . .

And cast ye the unprofitable servant into outer darkness: there shall be weeping and gnashing of teeth.

Matthew 25:30 KJV

Errol, Errol, Errol...
Where do I start? Well...

I HAVE A DOOR. It may be the best thing about my job. The only reason I get a real office, one of the few left with actual walls and a door, is that because I work in Human Resources, I am in the secrets business. Employees come to me to confess, to accuse, and to plot. That may strike you as titillating, being the host of the corporate reality show, but no. Not at all. I wish we had more idiots like those on television shows, the ones so stupid as to tell the whole truth. I get only truthlettes, little self-serving pieces, candy-coated and...

Hold on. In my eagerness to begin I realize you might be confused as to why I'm going on like this. It's because I got an email from your mom saying that you have decided upon a career in Human Resources. A lot of college kids think that because, like you, they "enjoy working with people." Hey, Mr. People-Person, drive a sno-cone truck if you want. Just don't look to HR.

Because you are now in just your junior year I figure I have time to show you the light and persuade you to pick some other specialty within your business major. I tried explaining my career when you were home at Thanksgiving, but I hear that I failed to dissuade you. So I decided that I'll show you what the HR life is like, using an online document to create a blog/journal to take you along with me as I do my job. I'll keep it going as long as I need to, but I'm guessing that in three months you'll write to me with tears in your eyes, thanking me for sparing you from a life of small victories and large defeats.

(The little blog that I'm creating is a private one, password protected. I thought about writing letters, but they're too slow; phone calls too problematic to orchestrate; email far too dangerous. I imagine you thinking, "Dangerous?" Oh yes, the stories I could tell—and will. Actual events, reflections and blunt commentary that would get me fired and banished from the profession. I take that chance because you are more a son to me than a nephew and I trust you to never repeat what you read. Are we on?)

```
USER ID: Win-Win
PASSWORD: ********
```

A Good Reason To Look Elsewhere

A S PROMISED, my life in HR, reported more-or-less as it happens.

Let me start with what you see after you pass through my office door and step into my office. There, right there in front of you is a good reason to look elsewhere for a career. You do NOT want to work in a job where you must keep a box of Kleenex next to the visitor chairs.

Here's an idea: I'm going to start a list of Reasons to Be Glad You Don't Work in HR, and that will be...

REASON #1: The box of tissues next to your visitors' chairs. (Who does that? Divorce lawyers? Grief counselors? Look at those two zippy, upbeat careers and see if that's the company you want to keep.)

I just got interrupted by my first visitor of the day. Not yet 7AM, and already I have a visitor. One of the Old Sweats. I'm not sure what that term means, but I read it in a British novel and it fits the old guys who work here. I'm on my way to being one of them now, deep into my forties, so I have a special affection for the office greybeards, especially this one. Reggie is a skinny guy with a shaved head who is 73. You wouldn't know he was in his seventies except for that mocking little tattletale of neck flesh, publicly losing its battle with gravity. He works out before coming to the work and still gets here before seven. He arrives in his workout clothes, which would be scandalous if he weren't 73; instead, they are just revolting. I try not to look at his crotch because most days he wears a pair of spandex bike shorts that must have been made from the original run of spandex in the nineteen-fifties or whenever. Inside those old shorts his manhood lurk-sags. I like the word you young people have: junk. Reg has major junk, and it takes an effort not to look at it, there against his thigh like he's shoplifting a travel umbrella.

"What are you doing here so early?" he asks, blinking, acting surprised, wanting to make sure I check the time and notice how early *he's* at the office.

"Work, work, work."

"Well, I'm glad you're here because I need you to level with me, man to man." Here he moves in conspiratori-ally and leans on the edge of my desk, in his right fist a small white workout towel, reminding me of last year's great shower debate.

(This is perfect... a telling little story about life in HR...

We have a shower facility in our building, not because our CEO supports employee fitness, but because it was there when we took over and it was cheaper to keep it. Naturally, it has become a source of constant problems, and not with plumbing.

REASON #2 to be glad you don't work in HR: You've heard that old line "No good deed goes unpunished." In our profession there's a corollary: No employee benefit goes uncriticized. (Should you think you've designed the perfect benefit, one you'd swear was so generous, so kind and good that it must be above questioning, think again;

you will inevitably have employees come to you and say, "Could I just have the money instead?")

Having showers is what enables guys like Reggie to bicycle to work and turn up at work in his deplorable shorts. The debate came after complaints about his showering and shaving in the locker room. Not employees griping about his using the locker room for morning rituals—others do it without complaint—but how he walks naked to the row of sinks, sets down his razor and Foamy, then he hoists up his manhood and lays it down on the counter like a sleeping ferret. No one wants to use the sink after that. *There should be a rule! they demand. A policy, for heaven's sake!*

What do you say to complaints like those? Do I sit down with Reggie and discuss his shaving posture? Let's go ahead and make that...

REASON #3 to be glad you don't work in HR: Reggie's junk.

And that brings us to...

REASON #4: Pretending to take seriously every stupid little issue brought to you by stupid little people. Or, better yet, let's put it this way...

REASON #4: All the occasions you MUST NOT LAUGH.

In this case, I couldn't laugh at the people who brought the matter to me... well, I admit to having laughed the first time, but then I caught myself and burbled out a quick, "Sorry, it's not funny," even though holding in my laughter made my eyes sting.)

But back to this morning: Reggie leans over my desk, glancing toward the door, and says softly, "Is it true that the company is moving?"

"Don't worry about it," pairing it with that look where you pull back like you smelled something foul.

I say that to Reggie even though I am myself worried—after all, Mr. Cone would transport his ailing mother to a nursing home in Mexico to save a few dollars a month. (True story.) But we've been through the threat of moving four times in five years. Each time I've told everyone not to worry because I don't want a rush of job searching. The employees who could most easily find another job are the ones you most want to stay, those with real talent or who are underpaid and don't know it.

Reggie is the VP who runs our warehouses and is a bargain. The Old Sweats often are if you're smart about hiring. They had careers somewhere and got laid-off, maybe more than once. Reggie has that work ethic that comes from parents who grew up in the Depression and had to decide whether or not to eat the dog. They decided not, he told me one night over a Bud Light, but it changes your relationship with pets for two generations, and as a byproduct, you don't take your income or your job for granted. Reggie outlived two wives and with his daughter living in Canada, the job is his life. He lowers his head so our faces are only inches apart. "You know what this job means to me, right?"

I vibrate reassurance.

"I'm a survivor, Win," he tells me gently. "Two tours in Nam, two cancers, two wives, and eleven lay-offs, not counting that reapply-for-your-job thing you pulled last summer. What do I have to do this time?"

"You're doing it, Reggie. Your group is putting up terrific numbers."

"Do I need to cut more costs?"

"That's always a good idea, Reg. But everyone agrees that you've done a fabulous job. Fabulous."

He glances around before a conspiratorial pronouncement: "Nobody is indispensible except the guy who decides who's dispensable. I have my list ready."

I'm glad I don't work for Reggie, because I'm sure I'd be on his list, and so would my box of Kleenex and everything else in what Reggie still calls Personnel. That makes him sound like a jerk, but I appreciate his old school approach to management, including the conviction that sending a problem employee to me would be weak and unmanly.

"Who do you want in your foxhole?" he asks me, and I truthfully reply, "You, Reggie, you." Nothing in my gaze betrays the fact that I have seen the CEO's own list of management dispensables and Reggie is number six.

He smiles like I'm a prize pupil, winks, and turns to go. I try not to look at his skinny ass but can't help but observe that it's firmer than my own. Without turning, he asks, "You're checking out my ass, aren't you, Cheeseley?"

I blush vividly and am grateful he keeps walking. And that brings me to…

REASON #5 to be Glad You Don't Work in HR: Being a man in a female-dominated profession means that your sexuality is constantly questioned.

You Must Be the Grandpa

I SHOULD START today's entry by explaining that I've been rethinking that last item from yesterday. As you know, people often assume that I'm gay. Because it never bothered me, I've always gone along with the jokes. Who cares? The truth is that I'd be happy to be part of that culture... I'd fit in... except for... well, except for not being gay. Correcting the misperception only matters to me now because I have become committed to finding a wife and having children. (Think of this: If I fathered a child today, I'd be in my sixties when he or she graduated from high school. I can imagine the "You must be the grandpa" remarks and shudder for the sake of young Winslow Jr. or sweet little Winslowia... or should it be Winslette?) So I'd like to be taken seriously as a potential heterosexual mate, a man's man in the *old* sense of that expression—that is, a ladies' man. I've resolved in recent months to change my image and to be more assertively hetero.

That resolve has forced me to understand that I have not been particularly *un*-gay. I'm an unashamedly fastidious man, and I'm single in my forties and that would be enough to pump the rumors. But it may be that working in HR is by itself considered sexually questionable, like being a florist. The field has a large percentage of women, but that's not the root of the problem. The real issue is that much of the job is feminine. Well, no, not feminine, not female... it's *maternal*. That's it. I'm the good sensible spouse who makes sure the children are just fine while dad goes out and hunts. I solve the domestic problems and make sure that Billy doesn't hurt Suzie's feelings and that the holiday party is sweet but not raucous. In a word, Mom.

Reggie assumes I'm secretly gay and being one of the Seen Everything People, he finds it mildly amusing but of no significance. And I admire the fact that at his age he assumes that he is attractive to me. More troublesome is the fact that our CEO thinks I'm gay and that creates alarming problems.

But I'm getting ahead of myself. You don't know about our CEO.

You probably remember that I work for a company called Mundane Industries, located in Phoenix. Most people think the company name is fictional, but Mundane Industries Corporation is our actual name, though we are usually known as M.I.C., pronounced Mick. The "mundane" name comes from the oddball sense of humor of our founder, Gerald "Genghis" Cone. (Don't think I'm going wild by mocking our founder; he likes being called Genghis, and has it included in press releases.)

The company is Mundane Industries because he created it to be a maker of me-too products. Our most successful items are middling-quality imitations. As Mr. Cone likes to say, we are a faux company. Let the glamour companies invest huge R&D budgets and do their test markets and their refinements and re-launches. We wait till a product is a success and then we move in, grabbing off a piece of the success. We have grown large and highly profitable, and that makes us a leader in not leading, if you follow me.

We work in a mid-rise building on the sagging outskirts of a declining warehouse district south of downtown. Mr. Cone is proud that we have the cheapest per-square-foot space in one of the cheapest cities in the country. We also have giant tax breaks because every few years Mr. Cone talks about moving to another city desperate for jobs and plays the offers of each one against the others. Nervous employees rush to me during these so-called secret relocation discussions, the ones that Mr. Cone always makes sure get into the newspaper. (He knows that while most people don't read the paper anymore, the people at TV stations do and the bloggers and tweeters watch TV. In a perfect media circle-jerk, the TV stations quote the bloggers and tweeters.) I'm one of the people who gets calls asking to confirm reports that discussions are underway to move the company, and my role is to act confused and say I can't comment because the talks are secret, which is how you tell them it's true in a way that gets them panting.

Our building's architecture fits our company name. Picture a brick laying on its long edge. Our particular brick is the color of river sand and rests in a desert of cracked asphalt. There is parking for 400 cars but just three reserved spaces, those three not just next to the building but covered, a big deal here in the desert sun. Mr. Cone takes the middle reserved space, leaving the others empty so no one will ding his car. I once gave Mr. Cone a copy of an article in which a company owner had started giving his reserved space to the Employee of the Month, and Mr. Cone responded by having "Reserved for HR Director" stenciled onto a space squeezed between the dumpsters and the chain-link fence. He was witty when he presented me with my new space. Honest. He has a sense of humor that many people don't get because he is absolutely dead-pan. Like when he suggested that we only hire tiny employees so we could have teeny little cubicles stacked two high. Just a joke but people got nervous, especially Big Connie in Customer Service.

As if the universe heard me reassuring you that I'm not gay, the best evidence of it just walked in and out of my office. Oh, my dear Errol, I confess that I'm a little shaky right now as I type this. She was wearing a short denim skirt and cowboy boots, an outfit that never figured into my fantasy life till now. I am lovestruck and have been for 321 days since I first interviewed her.

I can't mention her name, not even here. So let's call her Eve. Oh, how I yearn to bite her apples! (Was that too creepy? I'm opening up here, but there should be limits. Let me know.)

There's something about her, like she's about to make a dirty joke, although she never does. Freckles on the bridge of her little nose and... where else? If only I could survey that perfect skin.

She joined the company as an administrative assistant in Engineering, but now she reports directly to Mr. Cone as a Special Assistant. Don't ask me what that job title means. It wasn't in the handbook or on the Org Chart, but Genghis created the job the week after he first spotted her and started asking questions. I go crazy jealous when Genghis flirts with her. I lecture him on how inappropriate it would be to have any involvement with her, and he just chuckle-snorts like an old bull about to walk down the hill.

This morning Eve came by to tell me that Mr. Cone wants to see me at nine. Why not a call or text or email? Could it be that she wanted to see me, to drop in and chat? She flirts with me, although I know this is more her personality than an invitation, but she is not all that much younger than I am, less than a decade, and we always like the same movies. Is that enough? I think so. I get that vibe.

However, it is verboten to date anyone at any level below your own. So the only way I could date her is to get her fired or get her promoted four times. Anyone else in the company could just press ahead, keep it a secret for a while, then get married, or one or the other could find another company. Not me.

Let's make that ...

REASON #6: Always setting a good example.

Humphrey the Dead Cat

P EOPLE WHO MEET GERALD "Genghis" Cone are often surprised to find that he doesn't look like someone who would head a corporation. Passing him on the street, you might guess he was an Assistant Night Manager at Denny's. He is short-ish and wide-ish, and his arms are too long and skinny for his body, and his features are too small for his face, as if somebody assembling him misread some part numbers. He has disciplined himself to sleep just four hours a night, and perhaps this explains why his eyes are always puffy. Whenever he isn't talking or writing, there's a cheap plastic mechanical pencil between his teeth, held like a knife, giving him the look of an accountant pirate... which, come to think of it, defines his career rather well.

When I showed up at his office this morning, he took out the pencil and pointed it to a chair. I sat, and he said, "I need you to do two things. First, how many resumes and applications do we get a day?"

"Nobody counts them, but I'd say it's in the hundreds. You want me to get a tally and..."

"Who cares. What I want is for you to take the ones that come in the mail and print out the ones that come via email and put them in the lobby in a pile next to the elevators. You see the genius of that?"

I hate to admit it, but yes, I saw the genius of it—arriving and departing employees would get a vivid reminder of how many people were waiting to step into their jobs.

But now I had to puzzle out if he was serious or this was another of his jokes.

"It would take a lot of paper," I responded, stalling but knowing how he hates to waste any resource.

He tapped a pile of papers on his desk taller than the three paperback novels he had stacked on his desk awaiting his upcoming overseas flight. "This is how many inquiries have come straight to me in the last few weeks. Not all of them, just the ones about HR." He picked off the top sheet, no doubt carefully selected for grisly impact.

"Here's one from a cheery woman named Linda. She writes, 'Let me get right to the point, because that's the type of person I am: If I were running your Human Resources department, I would cut your employee costs by 20 percent. And I'm willing to work without pay for the first three months to prove it.'"

He gave me a lupine gaze over the top of the paper. "What do you think of that?"

Intentionally misunderstanding (an important corporate skill), I replied thoughtfully, "I have to say that it's a powerful opening sentence. Not possible to implement, of course, but it still gets you to the second sentence, which is the purpose of any letter's first sentence."

"I got to the second and third and all the rest, but that part about working for free was what I was asking about."

"You get what you pay for," I said, accustomed to his games.

"Ha! I have built this company on giving people what they didn't pay for—a brand name experience without the brand name price. "

"And that's just what you have in me, sir."

"You mean an imitation HR Director?"

"No, the real thing without the fancy packaging. Besides, who else would you enjoy tormenting as much as you do me."

"True. But just having seen this stack of resumes on my desk, I bet you work late tonight, and I bet that driving home you wonder how you could cut the size of our payroll."

He was right, but I knew better than to show weakness. "I always work late and I'm always thinking of how to cut our payroll."

He moved his lips in what may have been a smile and said, "Start collecting resumes and put them in the lobby as soon as you get an impressive mound, say ten thousand."

"I'm guessing this is your wickedly dry sense of humor, but if not, perhaps this is something we should kick around a bit and think through the possible unintended consequences. Is this really win-win?"

"Yes it is. I count on you to get it done, Cheeseley."

"Always, sir. But I need to point out that your reputation may take a hit." Even as I said it, I knew it was a mistake.

"You know that I carefully manage my reputation, and like most people, you can't help but believe that I'm a man who wants to be loved. If I wanted to be loved, I'd teach elementary school. Or go into HR." He looked at me, realized to whom he was talking, and added with a phlegmy snigger, "But then I'd have to kill myself."

He chewed his mechanical pencil for a moment, turning his face upward, lost in thought rather than seeing the cheap Swiss-cheese ceiling tiles. He was reaching that stage in his career where he enjoyed philosophizing about work as a way of talking about himself. "When I started out, I was a pal to everyone who worked here. At least that's how I saw myself. But after a while I figured out I wasn't really a pal. More like the rich uncle who could solve everyone else's problems. Think of that, Cheeseley: ten people's problems, bad enough, but then the company grows and you have twenty people's problems, then a hundred, then two hundred, and on and on. The better I got at solving problems, the more problems I got. Precedents were set: If I could give John a week off because his mother died, then I could give Julio a week off when his daughter was sick, and if I could give Julio a week off when his daughter was sick, then I could give Tina a week off when her cat died. And that really happened, back before your time, the thing with Tina and her cat. I even remember the cat's name: Humphrey. Tina was one of those people with twenty photos in her cubicle of this enormous cat, and I believed her when she said that Humphrey was her family. I gave her a day off, not a week, and she resented me for it. A day off, with pay, for a cat, and she resented me. That's when I came up with this realization: If you always say no, they eventually stop asking."

He leaned forward to add, "That's also when I hired my first HR person. That's been 22 years ago. That's your legacy, Cheeseley. You are a direct descendent of Humphrey the dead cat."

There are days I know just how Humphrey felt, but I didn't say so. Instead, I gently argued. "I just don't see why you'd want to incite animosity with all those résumés."

"To remind them that I'm a cheap, heartless bastard who doesn't value them."

"Even though it isn't true."

"Don't ever let me catch you saying something nice about me, Cheeseley, or you'll never write another employee handbook in this town."

That, by the way, brings us to …

REASON #7: You think reading an employee handbook is dull? Try writing one.

"Okay, then, Heartless Bastard it is." I stood.

He then paused as if actually thinking about what he wanted to say before speaking. "Another thing." Long pause. "It's about my daughter."

"I hear they love her in the Gilbert facility," I lied. This Carlota was an ill-tempered woman in her late thirties. Picture, oh, a peevish Newt Gingrich in drag.

"No, they fear her, which is better, but I don't want to talk about her work performance. I'm thinking bigger— her career. I want her to change her image. Right now, people think she's a lesbian."

I worked at looking startled.

"Oh, don't make that ridiculous cow face. They think that because she *is* a lesbian. And that's a problem with the Japanese investors I've been courting. So I want you to start dating her. You know, going with her."

This time the look of an alarmed bovine came without acting. Still, I regrouped, and with the lightning reflexes from decades of instantly making excuses for everyone's rotten behavior, I said smoothly, "Oh, but sir, as much as I adore Carlota and would enjoy spending time with her, there's a big problem."

"Don't worry. She knows you're gay."

"What? No, that's not it. I mean I'm not gay, but that's not the problem. We have those ironclad policies that we implemented as part of the settlement of the sexual harassment lawsuit, including the one about no dating."

He sighed. "Now I have to tell *you* what the policy says. It says you can't date someone at a level below your own. I thought of that and promoted Carlota this morning. She's now a Senior VP, just like you."

No. "In what job?" I squeaked.

"Head of manufacturing."

This was a disastrous move, morale-wise, and I might

have come up with some instant plan to head off the righteous indignation of the half-dozen more qualified execs, but faced with my own doom as Carlota's boy toy, I couldn't think straight.

"Call her," Genghis told me, "and invite her to the fundraiser at the Biltmore next week. I can't remember what damn charity it is, but she'll know. We'll get pictures of you two, and I'll have Regina get them in the papers and online."

Next he turned to holler to Eve to get someone or other on the phone, and I knew I was being dismissed. I should have argued, but then Eve walked in and my mind started shooting blanks.

Oh Shit, What a Mistake

WHEN I RETURNED to my office, one of my employees was waiting for me. Given my years of corporate life, I'm certain that I showed nothing and that he could not have known that my reaction to seeing him sitting in my office, which was, "Oh, shit, what a mistake I made when I hired this clown." I hired him just two months ago and I knew on the second day what a mistake I had made.

> **REASON #8: The person you interview is never the person you hire. And you are in charge of interviews.**

He came to me with two years of experience and seemed to be a person who could fill many of the holes in my department left by lay-offs and my female staffers being unusually fertile and perennially on maternity leave. Still I should have known better than to hire him when I learned that he had gotten a degree in HR. My first thought—and I burn with shame as I write this, but hey, Errol, you're the one who's thinking of a degree in HR—was, "Loser," followed by, "What sort of young man wants to enter that corporate monastery?"

Yes, those were my thoughts. Yes, the thoughts of the same man who was once selected Person of the Year by the Southwest Association of HR Professionals and might well have been National Person of the Year if the dipshit Secretary of the regional Association hadn't forgotten to attach the check for the admission fee and my application never got submitted to the committee. Yes, that selfsame me still saw a degree in HR and thought LOSER, God forgive me. If you fall into HR, that's one thing, but to seek it out as a young man with a world of possibilities, well, that's just sad.

Let's make that...

REASON #9: Lifetime Staffer Syndrome—when you choose HR as your field, you abandon all hope... hope of being rich or famous, or even head of the company.

This employee's name is Kyle, but because he claims to be one-sixteenth Apache, I have given him an Indian name: FullOfHimself.

To give credence to his supposed fealty to Native American heritage, he once offered to show me his tattoo of a "pollen trail," something about a bee following its symbolic path. Apparently that's something we humans are to do, too; we're to follow our pollen trail, meaning, he explained, to follow our true purpose.

I never did see the bee tattoo, because when I learned that it ran from his lower back down onto his hip and thus involved lowering his pants, I quickly declined. Still, the curiosity lingers: Where does the trail of ink begin and end? Such a mystery must be helpful when out on dates, moving things right to the pants-dropping stage.

The name FullOfHimself is just for my own amusement, never spoken aloud—after all, this Native American business is undoubtedly an attempt to get in on some minority status, and all of us in HR are doubly careful to be language straight-arrows when it comes to minorities.

(Speaking of arrows reminds me of a story. A true one.

A friend of mine was asked to give a speech to an organization of nuns. They had decided to do some cleansing of their language and taken out any reference to violence, especially any reference to battles, guns, or war. So you couldn't mention "taking shots" or "bullet points" or the "heavy artillery" or any of the other metaphors. I was conscious of it for a day, and it amazed me how many there were. Try it.)

As for FullOfHimself, he's tall and lean in a way that makes me think that he's not yet fat. His mouth is wide but his teeth are small, an effect like a row of white corn, and the whole oral assembly is in perpetual motion, as if the world can't wait to hear what idea just exploded in his brain, a human thought bomb. In just two months he has pitched me on giving him two major new projects, a promotion, and a raise. Just seeing him I want to snarl at him, "What do you want this time?" But no, I don't say that; I just smile and say, "What's happening, Kyle?"

"I had an idea that I think you're going to *love, love, love.* Here's my suggestion: That I get a certification. Put some initials after my name. Let people know that I'm not just the new guy but a solid professional. I know what you're thinking..."

This makes me smile because what I'm thinking is that I can't wait till the next layoff to correct this hiring mistake.

"...that any legitimate certification isn't free. But I found out they have a payment option so you could make it disappear into the expense budget."

We Cheeseleys are teachers at heart and I couldn't help but offer him a lesson in corporate reality. "Kyle, Kyle, Kyle. What I've learned in my career is that no one cares what initials are behind your name. They care that you care. They want to know that you've *listened.*" I leaned hard on that word and let it echo, which proved to be a mistake because he jumped in and started yammering about how it would really be to my benefit, and the company's benefit, to spend a thousand bucks for Kyle to gain additional training.

"First," I told him firmly, "there's nothing that disappears into the budget. There is no budget for such things, much less a magical disappearing one. Second, what you need now is to broaden your experience. You need time in the field, not in the classroom."

Clearly, he wasn't listening. He had a pad of paper in his lap angled so I couldn't see what was written there, but I suspected that it had notes from some article like "10 Tips for Successful Negotiation."

He then nodded as if agreeing with me and said, "I think this could be a real win-win." He knows my well-earned nickname is Win-Win, so he smiled as if he'd said something witty and I gave him a false good-one nod as I started to respond but he beat me to it, gassing on about how his certification would really be a huge advantage to me and that, looked at properly, a saint-like gesture on his part, helping me out.

This made me suspect that the article he'd been reading had a subtitle like "Get What You Want and Have Them Thank You for It."

A good manager knows how to say no, and I said it, gently but clearly. But that wasn't enough "no" for him. He retreated and regrouped, offering to split the cost. I studied his face, hoping for some comprehension of how annoying he was being, but zip, nothing there. That's why I've decided that I must give up on him as an employee. In his first weeks I devoted many hours to explaining to him how to be successful, but I could not get beyond his belief that it is my job, my duty, to help him get everything he wants and get it right away. Not just my job, but everyone else's too. It will take a hundred disappointments to convince him otherwise, and I gave him one, sending him on his way by glancing at my watch and doing the corporate version of cartoon eyeballs shooting out of the sockets on springs, then moaning, "Oh, my, look at the time—I'm supposed to be on a conference call."

That always works, the conference call bit. I once made the mistake of following the cartoon eyeballs by saying I was late for a meeting. But then I had to get up and pretend to actually go to a meeting and the other person said "I'll walk with you," so I had to walk around the entire floor and then the one below pretending to have forgotten which conference room the meeting was in. I wandered until I came to a meeting in progress and I slid in, apologizing, only to sit for a few minutes before doing a reverse slide and apology. This is not a problem with the faux conference call, where all you do is pick up the phone and pretend to be looking up a number till the person leaves your office. It has never failed me.

Good God, How I've
Learned to Lie

NEXT I DECIDED that I should go ahead and call Mr.
Cone's daughter Carlota and make arrangements
for our "date." Like her father, she answered the phone
not with hi or hello or "This is Carlota," but with a gruff
burst of just her last name, as if she was a curmudgeonly
detective on a cop show.

"Cone."

"Carlota, this is Win-Win Cheeseley. I just heard from
your father about your promotion. Congratulations. We'll
need to get out a press release." Big news! The boss's
daughter gets promoted!

"I have notes for you on a press release. Let's push the
fact that I'm the first female Senior VP, the youngest in
company history, and that I'm one of the most influential
female executives in the state."

Was that true? Doesn't matter. If that's what she
wants, that's what she'll get. It's not as though Anderson
Cooper would be assembling a panel to debate the point.

"I'll write it up personally."

"Good. Send it over. And thanks for the call."

"One other thing."

"Oh, shit. Look at the time. I have to be on a conference call."

"Just one sec. Your father mentioned being your escort
to the charity ball at the Biltmore next week."

"What? You? Father said that?"

"He mentioned it, and I jumped at the idea. I thought it was a terrific plan."

Good God, how I've learned to lie.

Let's make that REASON #10: Becoming a master liar.

She didn't say anything and I dared to hope that she'd put an end to the whole idea. I let the phone line hum while I silently pleaded with her to say that it wasn't going to happen.

With a sarcastic grumble she said, "So, you're asking me to be your date?"

And there she had me. Was it a date or just a corporate strategy session for the sake of the Japanese investors? And did she want it to be a date? Certainly not. But perhaps she wanted the honor of turning me down.

Striving for a note of insouciance, I said, "It'll be you and me and all the tony people of the Valley. I hear it's a lovely function."

Here was her chance to scoff, but there was more silence. I jumped in to paint a picture that I knew she'd find repugnant. She was a pants-suit, elastic-waistband type so I said, "You in a designer gown. Me in a tux. We dance. We drink champagne."

I leaned away from the harsh laugh I knew was coming. Instead, she giggled and purred, "Oh, I like it. I'll go shopping this weekend." Then, returning to her more normal, autocratic personality, added, "Get a limo. A classic one, not one of those stretch Hummers or something trashy." Then, ominously, she added, "And shave twice."

What? What?

Then the oddest thought occurred to me. Maybe she was no more a lesbian than I was gay. Maybe Genghis had it wrong on both accounts. And that would mean that it really was a date, the most unappealing woman in corporate America and me.

The Bullet Point

REASON #11: Having to fire people with gun racks in their pickup trucks.

THIS LATEST REASON in my list came to me because when I came into my office this morning and swung out my desk chair as I started to sit, I froze. There on my desk, centered on the edge nearest my chair, was a bullet, standing upright like a tiny rocket ready to be launched in my face.

When I was younger, I would have called the police. Now I know better. They would send out a pair of bored cops who would file a report, and some newspaper reporter would spot that report and write a story with a headline like "Exec Gets Different Kind of Bullet Point." What would that accomplish? The reporter would detail all the horrible things the company has done to employees, and I'd get a couple of semi-literate emails in support of my anonymous bullet provider arguing that "the world would be a better place without ass-wipes like you in it."

I've gotten hate mail before, and only one had really bothered me. Not having a wife or kiddies, the ones that threatened my family were almost laughable. But one letter came with a picture of my dog—it was my sweet old dachshund, Christmas, now gone. But not a whole picture; they'd torn off the head and sent me that. Creepy. For months whenever I got a package of a certain size delivered to the office, I wondered if I'd find the head of old Christmas staring lifelessly up at me.

Still, the bullet was somehow more violent, more real than mere words, and I felt I should do something. I could call Security, but in our case that was either a jumpy young man named Quinton who carried a foot-long flashlight as a substitute billy club (because he's forbidden to carry weapons) or a former football player called Horse who waddled and chewed sunflower seeds (because he's forbidden to chew tobacco). Finally, I settled on confiding in Reggie, the Old Sweat with the spandex shorts. After all, he had Semper Fi bumper stickers and liked to wear camouflage pants, and he was someone I had come to trust. I asked him to come to my office, explaining that someone had left me a bullet. I knew I had the right guy when his response was to ask, "Was it a bullet or a cartridge?"

Turns out that the bullet is just the part that shoots out the barrel of the gun, and the cartridge includes the casing and power. Now I knew that I had a cartridge, and that caused Reggie to growl and say he was on his way.

That gave me time to wonder what I would do with the thing. I hadn't thought about it having gunpowder in there. I could pitch it in the trash... well, place it carefully in the trash... but then what would happen when the garbage truck compressed the load. Would that set the thing off? Imagine reading that a trash collector had been shot by a bullet in the trash. Would I turn myself in? Then again, if I didn't throw it away, what would I do with it? Leave it lying around the office? Maybe set it on my bookcase as a warning to young people who wanted a career in HR? Hmmm.

Reggie soon put an end to my speculation by offering to take it to the gun range. But not before he offered his chilling analysis. "What you have there is .338 Lapua. A boat tail hollow point."

"Is that a good thing?"

Staring admiringly at it, he replied, "If you're a sniper, that's a first-rate ammo round. Some of our boys in Afghanistan used them."

And, so help me God, my training is so thorough and so complete that I corrected him. "We don't talk about them as being boys anymore, Reggie. It's men or women, and since in this case it could be either gender, it's *soldiers*."

"It would take one tough broad, but hey..." He shrugged as if he'd known plenty of tough broads.

"Woman, Reggie. Woman. But never mind about that. You're saying it's a sniper's bullet."

"Ammo, Win, ammo. And depending on the skill of the shooter, it has a range of oh, a thousand yards. Conservatively."

"Ten football fields?"

"If you don't count the end zones."

I pointed out the window at the neighboring buildings. "That one or that one."

"Relax, Cheeseley. If he knows what he's doing..."

"He or she."

He gave me a death-ray look that made me forget about gender-neutral expression, at least for a minute.

"If he knows what he's doing, he wouldn't chance a shot through glass. It would alter the course of the bullet. Now if he had left you a .308, what they call a tactical cartridge, that one's made to minimize deflection going through glass. Now *that* would be a statement about hitting you where you work. In fact, if he takes a shot at you while you're here in the office, that would be a good thing, because he'd probably miss and you'd know you were dealing with a dumbshit." His face let me know he'd just switched on a thought bubble. "But, hey, even then he's probably smart enough to wait a minute and see what you do. And what would that be? You'd hear the glass shatter behind you and you'd stand up and walk over to the window to see what happened, making for a nice clean second shot. You might want to practice diving to the carpet. Do it till you have it in muscle memory."

"So I'm probably okay in the office. That makes me feel better."

He worked his tongue around his teeth as if wanting to spit and said, "Well, you're safer in the office than walking in from the parking lot."

I got a mental picture of me doing a creep-trot staying below the roofline of other cars then a hunched dash to the lobby doors. Maybe I'd get a Kevlar vest. Given all the problems in Europe and South America, I wouldn't be surprised if they didn't make men's three-piece suits from bulletproof fabric.

Reggie added, "Or sitting on your patio or going skinny dipping in your swimming pool."

"Ay! Stop! So what would you do?"

"Well, I wouldn't go putting up rainbow decals and…" He stopped, shrugged, and said, "No offense," before adding, "but I certainly wouldn't wear a vest or sprint in from the parking lot."

"No, of course not."

"Leaving a cartridge is just bullshit posturing, especially a big round like this one. I'd rather be missed by a .45 than hit by a .22. So it's playground bully stuff." That gave me an excuse to do nothing, which is my favorite solution. I smiled and nodded, but that's when he added, "I wouldn't ignore it, though. I'd figure out who might do such a thing and let him know that if anything happens to me that he'd be taken out. Maybe rough him up along the way."

"Good Lord. So that's what *you* would do. What would you do if you were me?"

"Just what you're doing. Bring me in. Get together a list of who hates you, and we'll go over it together. "

"But I don't know that anyone hates me."

Another death-ray look. "Cheeseley, you've laid off or fired hundreds of people."

"Not by choice. And many of those people have thanked me. Besides, they know that it's just business. Nothing personal."

He blew out some air in little pa-pa-pas. "Come on, man. You get fired, you lose your income. You lose your income, you lose your self-respect and maybe your house and family. That's personal. A lot of those people look at the moment their lives were thrown onto the downward spiral, and who's there doing the throwing? You, pal."

"No, no. Not me. I don't think that's how people think."

"You remember when I took you to lunch for your birthday?"

"Very thoughtful." I had been touched that he knew my birthday and took the time to come by and offer to buy lunch.

"We went to Sal's and one of the waiters turned out to be a guy who used to work in Sales, a guy who had to be remembering the sweet job he *used* to have. And I decided not to eat. I told you I was having indigestion."

I nodded.

"It wasn't indigestion. I saw the hate in that guy's eyes and was afraid he was doing something disgusting to our food."

"No. Really? At least you could have told me."

"It was your birthday, and you were so upbeat and all that I didn't say want to spoil your mood unless I could see something suspicious on your food. I remember wishing you hadn't gone with the Creamy Parmesan dressing. The point is that I could see the deep anger in that guy. It was glowing. You were oblivious. I thought you HR types were supposed to be tuned in to emotion and body language and all that shit."

And there's a newly minted REASON #12: Not being able to eat out because the restaurant employees might be people you laid off.

Reggie went on to suggest that I get a list of everyone fired or laid off in the past few months, especially where I'd been called in to do the actual deed, and then we'd match that against gun ownership and criminal records.

"By the way," Reggie said, "it'll make things easier if you leave off the women. I know you want to be all fairsy-squaresy and all, but a woman would never be thinking of a sniper shot. She'd want to kill you up close, with a handgun or maybe a blade, or more likely just bitch at you till you killed yourself."

I covered my ears and hummed "America the Beautiful."
(Make that REASON #13.)

What Kind of Creep?

LATER THAT MORNING, still finding myself glancing out my window, looking for the glint of a sniper scope, I handled routine matters, and you might like some idea of what constitutes a routine HR matter. That day it was the case of the employee who'd repeatedly left work early to pick up his handicapped son who was "acting-out" at his special needs school. Then, by a series of coincidences, the manager found out that this employee had no children and was having an affair with a waitress who worked shifts at two restaurants and could only rendezvous from 2:30 to 3:30 in the afternoon.

I had to admire her energy. But I also had to make her Romeo choose between his job and his love life. He chose the job, which meant two more restaurants added to the list of places where I couldn't be sure what they were doing to my food.

Many people would be shocked—you might be among them—to hear that the manager and I let the lying Lothario keep his job. I mean, what kind of godawful creep invents a handicapped kid at a special needs school? However, we kept him on for our sake, not his. Replacing a good employee is expensive and time-consuming. This guy had taken work home and kept up his output, something someone with an actual handicapped child probably wouldn't have been able to do. So did we end up with a win-win? Yeah, but only by crawling through the basement window of the House of Practicality. Plus,

I have a soft spot for romance.

Speaking of negotiation, who popped into my office this PM but Kyle, the one I assigned the Indian name FullOfHimself. He curveted around my office door and said with faux bonhomie, "I just had a thought." I resisted saying, "Let me guess—was it about *you*?"

Sure enough, he was trying out another argument on why the company should pay for his certification. I'm sure that he's proud of being a "won't take no for an answer" guy and I know that he thinks of himself as a shrewd negotiator. What he doesn't yet know is that the best negotiators aren't shrewd.

I made an attempt to educate him by saying, "A couple of years back a technical guy came to me and boasted that he had gotten a big raise. He was very self-satisfied, bragging. Why? Because the week before he'd come to me to complain that he was underpaid and deserved a big raise and wanted my help. I took the trouble to explain that he was wrong, that he wasn't underpaid. I wasn't trying to con him—I had the statistics. He called me, quote, a tool of the system, unquote, and said he'd prove me wrong. I told him to be careful, that being overpaid was dangerous. Still, he went to his boss and threatened to quit. As he was working on a major new program, the woman he worked for gave him the raise."

Kyle nodded, identifying with him. Moron.

Then, the denouement: "Even before that raise had gone through the system and showed up in his paycheck, his resentful boss came to me for advice on starting a file." (I don't know if you know that expression, but that's what we call it when you begin to gather the paperwork to fire someone.) She told me that he was always pestering her about something and he just wasn't worth the trouble, much less the higher salary.

It was only then that FullOfHimself showed some interest in the story, and I was pleased to fill in the details. "But the manager didn't need the file, because within a couple of months, just after the project was complete, there was a lay-off and he was top of her list. He came to me—to me, the tool—and asked me to intervene. I explained that he was overpaid and thus the most vulnerable. He offered to go back to his old salary. Too late. All I could do was give him a check for two weeks' pay and this advice: The best negotiator is the one who knows when to stop negotiating."

I waited for that to sink in before asking FullOfHimself if he got the point. He proved he didn't by saying, "My dad used to always say, 'Don't leave money on the table.' He's the one who taught me that no matter what your job, you're in Sales."

"The best negotiator," I repeated, "knows when to stop negotiating. You don't just want to *get* a good deal; you want to *be* a good deal. Putting that philosophy to work is why people call me Win-Win and smile when they do."

I smiled. He smiled. Then he said excitedly, "Yes, I get it. That's why I stopped by—this certification is *such* a good deal for *you*."

I stopped smiling and said, "Oh, my goodness, look at the time. I'm late for a conference call." But what I longed to say was, "Oh, shut up! JUST SHUT THE FUCK UP!"

I've been wanting to say that for 23 years, which is exactly how long I have been in Human Resources, and that qualifies as...

REASON #14: Never being able to say JUST SHUT THE FUCK UP!

Riding a Horse Through the Hallways

KEEPING THIS JOURNAL has made me introspective. Perhaps I need to do more to change my image than trying to put an end to the rumors about my sexuality. What do you think? I play up the whole Win-Win thing, but maybe that's part of the problem. How far from win-win is wishy-washy? I wonder if it's possible to be a tough, macho HR person.

Right there in what I just typed is the problem—just now, ending that last sentence I tried to type in the closing word as "man" and couldn't do it... the whole gender thing.

It doesn't help that I'm a small man. At 5'7", I'm no midget, but it's a challenge to look up at someone and *loom*. I suppose Napoleon had it figured out. Maybe he spent a lot of time on a large stallion. If I could figure out how to pull off riding a horse through the hallways of the office... now *that* would surely change my image.

I just looked up heights online and discovered there's a site just for that purpose, which didn't surprise me as there's a site for everything. It might make for an interesting game to have people shout out topics *without* a website and see if there are any.

(We have a filter on the computers here at Mundane Industries that won't let employees go to any pages but the ones we have approved. I, however, have free access. Why? Because I have to give approval to sites, I have to be able to check them out. That means there's an item to put on the other side of the ledger when it comes to weighing a career in HR. That makes two on that side—the Internet access and the office door.)

Back to the site about heights. When I put in 5'7", I found a banner ad for "elevator shoes." Curious, I put in 6'6" to see what ads came up and... Elevator shoes. Apparently we wees aren't the ones obsessed about heights. And, no, I didn't click on the ad.

Not an inspiring group, the five-sevens. There's Salman Rushdie, Robin Williams, and Zach Galifianakis. You don't see those names and think Leaders of Men... I mean, Persons.

But then I spotted Duane Chapman, AKA Dog the Bounty Hunter. Not bad. And there's Vladimir Putin. OK, so there's a guy who knows how to lead.

Looking him up on the web, I found one site with a headline "50 Pictures of Vladimir Putin Looking Like a Complete Badass" and this intro paragraph:

Oh, I'm sorry. Were you planning on having peaceful talks with Russian Prime Minister Vladimir Putin? Yeah, go ahead and try your hand at diplomacy when he's shooting you with a harpoon. The guy's a total badass.

There are amazing pictures, amounting to a primer on how to come across as tough. The intro referred to a couple of photos where he's in some sort of rubber-raft/speedboat combo, brandishing a crossbow harpoon. Plus there are several where he's hunting, including squatting above a dead tiger. Too far for me to go, of course, but there's something to be said for whipping your shirt off when hunting or fishing. A lot of guys look like wading dork-storks when trout fishing, but Putin takes off the shirt and wears a foot long knife on his belt (just in case a shark swims up the river, I guess) and the result—yeah, oh yeah, badass. The best photos came from an indoor shooting range, where he's wearing a suit and tie and holding a pistol and your mind just barks out, Hey, James Bond. That's the perfect one for me. I even have the ideal excuse for joining a shooting club, what with having had that bullet—okay, cartridge—left on my desk.

So I've found my mental mentor. I'm going to start asking myself, What would Putin do?

No! Never!

I SHOULD EXPLAIN why I was going on about my image yesterday. It's this dream woman I was telling you about. My real motivation to go online to study Putin was because Eve called me and asked if she could stop in and "toss around an idea." You bet.

She came in wearing a belted dress of some silky fabric that was running its hands all over her. I came around my desk to sit beside her in one of my visitor's chairs and I was so intent on not noticing how her dress caressed its way up her thigh, that I hit my knee on my desk corner and let out a yelp of pain and doubled over into the chair. Not how I wanted to start with my new image. My new mentor, my inner Putin was on assignment and instructed me to "Bite a tampon, pussy. Never show pain."

We worked our way into the conversation. She commented on the latest gossip about some nitwit celebrity, or maybe it was the latest nitwit politician. Then, just as we hit the first silence, I dropped the lines that have served me so well in my work. "You seem like you have something on your mind. Am I right?" Sounds dumb, I know, but this is how I get employees who are working up to some embarrassing revelation or request to get to the point. Not that I was trying to get Eve to rush, but I knew she wouldn't relax till we got to the real stuff, and selfishly, I wanted to advance to that meaty layer of conversational lasagna where people start to know each other.

She puckered up with surprise. "Well, aren't you perceptive?" She was truly impressed, and I felt like a bit of a fraud even though magicians surely still feel like magicians despite knowing the trick.

I gave a half-smile and a half-nod that added up to a whole sincere.

"This is awkward," she began. "Can I ask you something off-the-record, just in confidence between you and me?"

The Human Resources profession has drilled into us an unusually clear and concise answer to this question: NO! NEVER!

That's because the employee is likely to reveal something that you are obligated to report. We aren't doctors or priests, despite doing parts of their jobs, so we can't offer legal protection when it comes to confidential information. Here, however, all my training was for naught. I urged her to proceed and tried to look a bit mischievous to let her know that by giving her my word I was breaking one of the commandments of my profession.

She saw my look and misread it. "Your knee! Poor thing. I could find some ice."

I told you she was an angel. I swiftly cleared up the confusion and urged her to confide in good old Winslow and heard my inner Putin mockingly repeat her "poor thing," then belching.

"I know what the Employee Handbook says on this subject. I looked it up. But I also know that there are written rules and then there are the real rules. I decided to come to the man who'd know them both."

I wanted to give a man-of-the-world chuckle, but then just as I was giving it voice, she smiled and it took my breath and the noise that came out was like something from a rubber dog toy.

Putin noticed; she didn't.

Shyly, she began. "Tell me the real story on what happens when a man and a woman…"

With a girlish grimace she left that hanging, leaving room for me to jump in. But I didn't trust my voice so I just gave the tell-me-more head-dip.

"This is just too embarrassing. There is someone, I think, someone in the company, an executive, who's interested in me, and I…" Again she lost momentum and again waited for me.

Putin offered guidance: "This is your moment, you lucky little shit. Take her hand. Lean in till you feel her breath on your face and tell her that you have adored her since the day you first saw her and that you'd give up everything for one night in her arms."

Not bad, but I found myself saying instead, "Ah, so you're asking about the company policy on employee dating?" Belatedly I reached over to take her hand, but she'd already leaned back and there I was with my hand flopping there between us till I ended up, who knows why, putting out my palm for a high-five.

Confused, she eventually responded with a limp mid-five pat.

I burbled on a bit about the history of the no-dating policy, the harassment lawsuits and so on. I heard Putin spit and say he'd had enough and that he was leaving and I could sense that any bonhomie, much less aura of flirtation, leave with him.

She broke into my monologue and said, "I understand the policy. But what happens if someone breaks that rule and gets caught?"

I wished that Putin had stayed around because he might have approved of what came next. I gave a knowing Marlon Brando in *Godfather* look of assurance and said, "In my position you can't come out and say that anyone is above the policies, but, then again, who's going to arrest the sheriff?"

This took her aback, but then she seemed to understand and leaned toward me and patted my arm. "Got it." She rose with the grace of a dancer and strolled out while I sat and felt my forearm then my cheeks grow warm.

Scarlet Satin

HAVE YOU EVER RENTED A LIMO? It's not something I do. Haven't done for many years, not since college, but because Carlota had insisted, I signed up for one, pointing out that I needed a normal limo, not a gaudy one. They sent a Lincoln Town Car, black, well maintained, but *not* a limo. The driver, who looked as though he spent his days in the weight room and acted as though he had faked his way through customer service training, told me that I'd ordered "limo service, not a limo" and had specifically requested what the company called "the low-key option," which his attitude told me he interpreted as the "cheapskate" option.

I debated out loud whether it was better to drive my own car or show up in this. "Your call, pal," the driver concluded without a touch of paly-ness. I got in.

We arrived a few minutes early at Carlota's condo and she yelled from behind the door that I was "fucking early" and left me standing outside for a few minutes and then after another shout, "Coming," a few more. When she finally stepped out, it was a shock. Around the office she wore clothes that a farm-town librarian would find too dull, leaning on the loose and the dark, the sort of outfits that one employee once described to me as "a wardrobe of sexual invisibility cloaks." (Well put, but I couldn't laugh, not in my position... see Rule #4.)

Tonight, though, was different. I had taken the time to script some at-the-door compliments to go along with a phony leer, knowing that this was part of the charade of our "date." The shock on my face and the "wow" on my lips were, however, genuine. Carlota had chosen a scarlet satin dress, daringly low-cut with an empire waist, ending above the knee, along with elaborate high-heels and elaborate high hair.

"This isn't a dental exam," she said, confusing me till she added, "you can close your mouth."

Using both hands I pretended to lift my jaw. "Can you blame me? This is a new you."

"No. It's an old me. I love dressing up, just not for work."

You might be asking yourself if I now found myself attracted to her and if this was the start of some surprise romance novel courtship. No. Setting aside the large breasts on display that night, she has the body of a tubby middle-aged guy, including the beer gut. More importantly, and far worse is the issue I mentioned earlier, that there is something of Newt-Gingrich-in-a-dress about her, masculine and with a gut, but moreso she had in her an angry condescending Newtishness that would make you want to vote for someone else, much less date someone else.

As we went out to parking area, I began to apologize for the Town Car, but she cut me off with a brisk "Not an issue."

I don't know if you've been to the Arizona Biltmore Hotel. If not, I must take you the next time you come to town. It's a Frank Lloyd Wright design, built in the 1920s but still managing to look modern, perhaps because the interior walls are made of unpainted concrete blocks with a palm-frond design, an industrial chic that feels much newer than the addition, a wing added in the last decade or two, featuring a WalMartization of the original FLW design, and which I feel certain, if he were ever to return and see it, he would happily burn to the ground and start over.

We were there at the Biltmore for a charity ball, an excuse for wealthy women to put on a prom. Genghis had been talked into buying a couple of tickets by some CEO pal and surely he was grateful for an excuse not to go, instead sending Carlota to let the event become the corporate version of a debutante ball. (Ironic, isn't it, that such balls used to be called "coming out" parties, but here Genghis was hoping to prove to investors that Carlota was *not* "coming out" in the new sense of that term. But, as I've told you, I'm not at all sure about her actual sexual preferences.)

Knowing that the point of our being in attendance was to have photos for the paper and, from there, for our corporate website and our investors, I made sure to give the photographer my card. I debated slipping him a couple of twenties, but decided that the business card was a better bet, especially when I added that we often needed photographers for our corporate functions. That worked, and he took dozens of shots of us, including several of us on the dance floor where I worked at gazing lovingly at Carlota in a hyper-hetero way.

There was one moment when I shooed the photographer away. Carlota had sent me to the bar several times for gin and tonics, and as she loosened up at one point she was working to scratch her back and the physics didn't work—she possessed more back than arm length. Being a gentleman, I offered to help and she ended up instructing me to unzip the back of her dress to get my nails under an elastic thing—what might be that reinvention of the girdle known as Spanx. It was a sleeveless dress so the zipper ended between her shoulder blades and the elastic undergarment started a couple of inches below the top of the dress. It was tight in there, like working to retrieve a quarter from the spot where the base and back of the car seat meet, but she moaned when I found the right spot, then she directed me to another spot, then another. I bit my tongue and worked on. She barked instructions and urged me to such animated scratching that I feared she might start bleeding, noting that her skin was surprisingly velvety, not unlike the plush seats on an old Chevy Monte Carlo I once owned.

Well, by and by I defeated the itch, and it was time to rezip. No problem in reclaiming the couple of itches where I had the aid of the elastic undergarment, but above that was a bulge, the sort of thing that I've heard you young people refer to above jeans as a "muffin top." What to do? I was tempted to just leave her dress a bit unzipped, but as soon as I pretended to be finished, the zipper began to wander south, trying to lessen its load. So I tried again, working to pull down with the fabric with the left hand while pulling the tab up with the right and simultaneously asking my right-hand pinkie to do some frantic muffin stuffing. Useless.

I gained a bit of time and distraction when some friend of Carlota's approached and after a brief introduction I was free to redouble my labors. The last thing I wanted to do was embarrass her by admitting that the zipper simply would not close, and the next to last thing I wanted to do was catch her Monte Carlo upholstery skin in the zipper and have her scream. Then I came up with a solution. We'd had an Italian dinner, and there on the table were miniature saucers of olive oil. I surreptitiously slipped a finger into the oil and worked it over the relevant square inches of skin, and just like that, the zipper climbed that last distance while I stifled a roar of triumph.

I confess to relating that story to you with pride,

believing it's a metaphor for the HR life; you find a way to grease the situation, to make things better, often behind the backs of those involved so that they don't even know what you've done. In this case, I say, "All done" and patted her on the back. My own back remained, as usual, unpatted.

Speaking of patting. We spent a lot of time on the dance floor, offering up a maximum number of photo ops. Carlota had on extreme heels and that made her taller than I am, and on the slow songs my face was worryingly close to the canyon of the cleavage. If I had let my face fall forward, it would have been like putting it in that circle pad on a massage table. After a few glasses of wine, I found myself tempted to let my neck muscles go and see what transpired; however, I am nothing if not a monument to self-restraint.

To distract myself, I turned to study the marauding ass of the lithe woman to my left. About that time, the band's drummer, sounding like a cowboy version of Barry White, crooned a song that Carlota found moving. I looked the song up later and it was called "Getting You Home" by Chris Young, about a couple getting dressed up and going out for the evening only to find that both can't wait to get home and get naked. They return home and there's this part about the woman's black dress falling to the floor. That line made Carlota purr. I continued to check out the ass off to the left and smiled when, glancing to make sure Carlota wasn't noticing, discovered that Carlota was watching the same divine ass.

As you may have noticed, I've been going to the gym and have developed a solid physique, including the surprising midlife appearance of the chest muscles known as pecs. We'd been dancing a while at this point, and I was getting a tad humid with the exertion, making my shirt soft. While I was checking out the woman dancing beside us, Carlota reached a hand inside my tux jacket and pinched a nipple. I pretended it hadn't happened, as if it were possible to tweak a nipple by accident. Then she pinched the other one. Naturally, they stood up to see what was going on. Carlota turned back to me, and I looked away as she let her fingers dance across one rigid nipple and then the other and whispered into my ear, "Two out of three." Then she started her fingers walking south and Lordhavemercy as I realized her destination I noted that I was well on the way to three out of three. The song ended as her fingers walked over my cummerbund but she reached down for a quick confirmatory squeeze.

I've been to a lot of seminars on body language, even taught a few, but you don't need my certification in non-verbal communication to figure out what's being said when your pecker jumps up and says, *Let get the party started!* The traitor.

She gave me an "aren't-you-naughty" face, and I whipped off my jacket and draped it over my arm, which made her giggle as we walked off the dance floor.

Neither of us was sure what to say, and she stopped a passing female exec to chat while I tried to convince my erection to save itself for another day. That's when my inner-Putin decided to pop by and offer congratulations, chuckling before commenting. "The manly genes inside of her are just what your wimpy genes lack and they know it." He lit a cigarette, then added, "Your genes are instructing your pecker. That is the real language of love." Then he laughed. "Just don't expect me to watch."

Before I could respond to the imaginary dictator, Carlota turned to me. "This is someone you should meet. This is..." and I thought she said "Missy Grey-Black," her given name being perfectly ill-suited to her demeanor. She was a hard-looking woman who gave me such a sinister and judgmental look that I immediately wondered if I'd once fired her. Something about her made me think of that bullet on my desk.

Always the gentleman, I gave the slightest bow and said, "My pleasure, Missy Grey-Black."

She snorted. "It's not Missy. It's *Ms.* Ms. Roberta Grey-Black." And her attitude added, "Asshole."

Carlota studied the two of us as if deciding which one to bet on. Well, maybe I'm projecting that onto her because of what I later learned.

Ms. Grey-Black turned back to Carlota and switching on all the lights in the house of her personality gave her an overlong embrace and said she'd see Carlota the next week and walked off.

"Who was that?"

"She's a consultant with... oh, I've had too much to drink... the one that does HR outsourcing...Wise and Regatta?"

"What?" I squawked, any remnants of my stiffy reversing in alarum. The words "HR outsourcing" and "Wiseman and Regary" are the last words any HR exec wants to hear. There is a movement among corporations to have an outside company "hire" all its employees and thus handle all the payroll and paperwork. The result is that W&R takes over the complete Human Resources function. This would be the end of my department and thus the end of the employment of one Winslow "Win-Win" Cheeseley. Carlota gave me a pout that might have been sympathy. "I don't think Dad has made any decisions." She cupped my left pec and said, "Besides, I need you around to be my big, strong, straight man," and she gave me a surprisingly gentle kiss, just a tad slower and wetter than lady-like and my poor wanger turned over, puzzled.

HR Summer

REASON #15 to be glad you don't work in HR: The first day of HR Summer.

THERE'S A DAY that every HR person learns to dread, and I've come to think of it as separate from Summer itself, which explains the "HR Summer." Here in the desert it comes early, in March or April, and it is the first hot day of the year, the first day that employees decide they should wear something cool in the original sense of that word. That's the day we get calls from conservative employees or managers who are shocked by the newly exposed flesh but lack an acceptable corporate vocabulary for reporting offenses. "She walked in wearing a pair of shorts so small that I can see her... see her... well...too much."

Our department is a very "lean" operation, which means that most of the middle manager positions have been eliminated, so the work of those middle managers has been spread up and down; that's why I got a visit from FullOfHimself, who came to complain about his role on the first day of HR Summer.

(For the following exchange to make sense, I have to back up and tell you that Eileen is another of my employees, slightly senior to FullOfHimself in age but not rank; she is, however, much more politically adept.)

"I hate to bring this to you," FullOfHimself lied, "but I knew you'd want me to be open about my feelings."

Wrong, but I said nothing.

"Eileen has been dividing up bare skin issues and she's really taken unfair advantage. She's basically keeping all the complaints about the young women to herself and all the complaints about the old women and the men to me. And I outrank her, technically."

"You should be grateful. Those are the easiest to deal with." This was my own counter lie, a gift basket of sour oranges. The saddest conversations are with older women trying to look young. Spend enough time in my HR shoes and you start to see the wisdom of burkas. (Hold on. I take that back. If I ran an office of burka-ed employees, there would still be the Brittany Spears of the office, going sockless and flashing some toe-cleavage and then complaining when the old guy in Distribution with the hairy ears stops to stare.)

And it's not just the women. Try having a serious conversation with some guy about how much of his chest or underwear we don't want to see.

FullOfHimself then offered a suggestion. "Somebody calls in a complaint, and then I have to schlep over to that department and be a voyeur and write up some assessment. Think how much faster it would be if they just took a cell phone photo and sent it to me."

"No, no, no. Remember, we have to think a step ahead. Always consider how anything we do would look if written up in the paper by a hostile reporter. And you have to assume all reporters are hostile because they succeed by making us fail. How would you like to have your mother read a story about how you have a collection of photos of employee's cleavage and butt cracks. They'd call you the Crack Police or some such. What would Mom think of that?"

"Couldn't we just force the managers to deal with their own problems?"

"Then we face the issue of an employee walking down the hall and going from Acceptable to Unacceptable just by walking from one manager's department to the next."

"Yeah, okay. But, hey, we could do a series of photos and put them on the website showing clothing that is Acceptable and Not Acceptable. Then let the managers enforce it."

I replied wearily, "But by publishing photos showing the Not Acceptables you're violating your own policy. And you're doing it in writing."

Defeated, he stood. "Hello HR—home of the Prude Patrol."

For me, while I didn't handle the petty complaints about dress code violations, I still had to act as judge when a manager or employee insisted on appealing some punishment handed out by the likes of FullOfHimself. So the start of HR Summer came at a bad time, as I wanted time to plan my response to the possibility of the HR outsourcing, and also I had scheduled time to discuss how to deal with the bullet/cartridge on the desk.

I finally got myself free from the day's troubles and called Reggie to join me in my office. He turned up wearing a pair of loose camo pants, along with a tight polo shirt, just showing off. His eyes were red, as if he'd been crying, but I have trained myself not to ask.

REASON #16: Being a good listener.

(You hear the sad stories, not just about the workplace but about every manner of heartbreak, and you and your squeezed heart have to sit there and listen and listen and listen. I mean how can you cut someone off with some pro-company HR-speak like, "I'm sorry your ten year old has leukemia, but that only makes your job and insurance more vital, so make sure you don't miss any work time, and remember, sick time is not about anyone else's sickness, just your personal sickness." And when you can't cut someone off, it wrests hours from the important work of HR, talent acquisition and management, which in the end becomes your sad story of all the things you never tried and the HR Executive of the Year Award you never won.)

A Path of Career Destruction

"GOOD GOD, WIN, you have left quite a path of career destruction." Reggie held up a stack of papers, then set it on the edge of my desk before turning and closing the door and pulling one of my visitor chairs up so we could look together at what he'd brought.

I knew he was carrying a list of those we'd been forced to fire or lay off, and my initial reaction to his comment was to defend myself and turn the blame on "Genghis"; but in this, as in all things, I bit my tongue.

(Biting the tongue like it's a piece of Juicy Fruit is an important corporate skill, and while especially useful in HR, I won't make it one of our official Reasons, because everyone should learn it.)

I said a vague "How's that?"

"I've been going through these data and trying to figure out ways to cut down the number to something reasonable, but shit, there's a lot here. We could use a posse, Sheriff."

"Perhaps we could get some help from Security, but..."

"Dumb and Dumber? Are you nuts?"

This is a measure of the fevered state of my anxious brain that I responded by indulging in a blatant criticism of these two, something I never ever permit myself, blurting out, "They are, I admit, sub-optimal, efficiency-wise." Reckless, I know, but there it was.

"Efficiency-wise? How about intelligence-wise or confidentiality-wise?"

"Then you see why, for now at least, that this is just you and me."

"And this is what we're up against." He pulled a pale yellow legal pad from the stack and began reviewing the numbers on it. "As I mentioned before, I left out the women for now, leaving eighty-seven men fired in the last eighteen months."

"I only know of a handful who were fired. You must mean that they were let go, right?"

"Let go," he repeated before making a coughing sound like a bike chain coming off the sprocket. "You mean *let go* like captured eagles yearning to be set free."

"Scoff if you will," I responded defensively, "but over eighty-percent of people who get laid off end up believing it was a good thing."

"Did you make that number up?"

This astounded me. "Yes. How did you know?"

"Never mind. Back to the point, which is how I whittled down the number to look at. There are three who died since being fired. There were also fifteen I couldn't account for, so I have to set them aside for now. There are also eight guys who I judged to be homosexuals that we can leave out."

"What?" I blurted defensively. There's something about so often being assumed to be gay that has given me a kinship. This makes me hyper-sensitive, which of course only convinces people they are right in their presumptions about me.

"Yeah, the gays, although none of these guys seemed very cheery to me."

"Naturally we don't keep records on such things. We don't even know anything about their sexual orientation, unless there's a harassment complaint. And if we did, what makes you think a gay man would not be capable of putting a bul... cartridge on my desk?"

"On both counts, just trust me. And let's hope that you get glitter-bombed instead of shot."

I tried to object, but he skillfully cut me off and pressed ahead. "Also, and this was the biggest help of all, there are twenty-four of our initial list who have moved away. Relocated. I don't see someone making a trip back here just to put a cartridge on your desk."

"Makes sense."

"So that leaves nearly forty on our initial list of suspects. Far too many. So I checked on their employment status and found twenty-four who don't have new jobs. Of those, eleven are calling themselves unemployed, while five say they've retired and eight are calling themselves consultants. I'm putting those eight at the top of my list to follow-up on."

"I don't see why."

"Consultant is a euphemism for unemployed. These are guys unwilling to admit that they weren't snatched up by some other company and know they're going to be unemployed a long while. They're the kind to sit and brood."

I shrugged, willing to just sit back and go along with Reggie's logic.

"Then there are those who have taken other jobs. Of those, I tried to isolate those who had to take a big step down in pay and prestige. There weren't very many, just ten, which confused me till I remember that coming from here it wasn't as far to fall." He looked up, checking to see if I was offended, but I had my shoulders loosened now and gave him another of my man-of-the-world shrugs.

"You hurt your neck?"

"No, I'm fine."

"So we have the eight consultants, the eleven unemployed and the ten worse off. I'm calling those our first targets, in that order."

"Excellent work, but that's twenty-nine people just for starters. Wouldn't it be easier to just find out who owns guns?"

"This is Arizona. You don't have to register a gun. You don't even have to have a permit to carry a concealed weapon, not since 2010."

"No. Can that be right?"

"Hey, it wouldn't matter anyway. The gun you worry about most is the one that isn't registered and can't be traced to the shooter."

"Bought on the black market."

"In the movies they call it a throw-down piece, one you just leave at the scene. That's how you tell law enforcement that they're dealing with a pro."

"So how can we possibly screen twenty-nine people, especially if we can't even let them know we're screening them? Impossible."

"We start with background checks, but then we get creative."

He did an eyebrow waggle that made me instantly wary. "Hold on. There can be nothing illegal. No breaking-and-entering. No roughing up anyone. Nothing like that."

Light flashed off his shaved head as he dropped it enough to turn his eyes up and give me a look that managed to say, "You disappoint me—you don't hurt or offend me because I'm far too manly to feel either of those emotions, but you definitely have failed to live up to my expectations." Perhaps I was reading too much into a look, but I think not.

"We get creative," he repeated, as if I were just a slow pupil.

Just then there was a knock, and Eve opened my door. "Sorry to bust in, but Mr. Cone has been trying to call you. He wants to see you right away. He was..." She searched for the right adjective. "…insistent. And he seemed upset."

Reggie rose and said to me, "Good timing. I need coffee." To Eve he added, "Can I get you a cup, Beautiful?" And they left together, his arm around her shoulder. Was she leaning into him? I told myself that I had no time for petty jealousies and I hustled off, nervously doing the hand-cup breath check and patting at my hair.

I Ask You, What Do You Say?

"I HAVE HERE THE PICTURES of you and Carlota at the benefit dance," Genghis began, working through several dozen eight-by-tens he held near his face, the white photopaper backs to me. "And I just can't believe what I'm seeing. Can you believe what I'm seeing?"

Not having seen any of the photos, there was no answer for that. I gave a politic response, "Carlota is special."

This drew a dark chuckle. "I guess so. You know that Rolling Stones line in "Start Me Up..." (Mr. Cone is full of surprises; who knew he'd be quoting Mick Jagger?) "... the one about the woman who could make a dead man come." (This staggered me, but you would never know it from the knowing half-nod that I returned.) "I don't think of Carlota that way, but here you are, a gay guy, and still you're staring down at her tits and sporting an obvious boner. Whoopee." He handed up a photo as he sang in a surprisingly crisp voice, "She makes a gay man hard."

The photographer had captured that instant just after Carlota tweaked my nipples and swagged my crotch, the moment just after I'd gotten aroused while watching the young woman dancing beside us.

I ask you: What do you say in that situation, being handed such a photo? Do you say, "Oh no, sir, you daughter is totally unappealing—I was half-drunk and fantasizing about the young woman next to us, who I now see was probably a teenager." No.

Blushing so furiously that I expected sparks to fly from

my nose, I managed to respond. "Maybe now you'll stop thinking I'm gay."

He waved that off. "We all are somewhere along the continuum, aren't we?"

That sentence, with it broadmindedness, startles me now, but at the time, all I could do was think of some apology. "I shouldn't have had the champagne. If you want me to go into therapy, I will."

"Stop sniveling. This is perfect. Perfect. The Japanese are coming in next week, and I'll find a way to let them see the photos. That'll put an end to the rumors about Carlota. They'll think that no self-respecting lesbian would let some pervert hang on her like that, and that'll be enough."

This was good news on one hand, but there's always that *other* fucking hand—viz., the picture of me and my boner would be hanging around the office for anyone, and especially for Eve to see and with social media it could be around the world in a Silicone Valley minute. Against this, I had to admit that Carlota's tug on my pants and the camera angle had been generous to my boner... but NO! the drooling eyes were just all wrong. Intolerable.

"I understand your thinking, Mr. Cone, but why risk offending our Japanese friends, and Carlota, indirectly. I'm sure there are plenty of photos that are less..." It was my turn to struggle for a work "...provocative..."

He cut me off. "No, these guys are wonderfully sexist. They'll love them. Just right. You're more of a man than I thought, Cheeseley."

"If I could just..."

He swiveled in his chair. "I've got a conference call." He turned his back, still holding the photos, not even bothering to pick up the telephone and pretend. I was left to wonder how it was that the photo could be used to confirm that Carlota was not a lesbian but could not do likewise and confirm that I was not gay. After all, I was the one with the leer and the boner. It's just not fair.

Ironic. That whiny little "not fair" sentiment has been thrown at me a thousand times in the course of my work, and I invariably respond by gently reminding the speaker that fairness is a concept best left unexplored, perhaps intoning in a throbbing voice, something like "Life isn't all carrots." That conversation gem suggests that it's sometimes about the rougher half of the carrot-and-stick formula, but when I cut it short at "Life isn't all carrots," it's so confusing that it's like hitting a conversational Reset button.

As I glumly walked back to my office, I told myself the bit about carrots, and guess what? I felt a bit better.

A Nifty Little Sting Operation

THAT MOOD DID NOT SURVIVE the walk back to my office. There, outside my own doorway, were Reggie and Eve, standing much too close, clearly violating the 18-24 inches of personal space that we were trained to give a colleague, but much worse, she had her arm outstretched fingering his shaved head. What is it that makes women so attracted to shaved heads? They are the opposite of a puppy or kitten or something you want to pet.

The pair were too engrossed in the wonders of Reggie's cranium to notice me so I said loudly to Eve's back, leaning in toward her left ear, "Mr. Cone was looking for you." This did not result in the dramatic straightening and restraightening of postures that I would have deemed appropriate, but instead, she invited me to join her in finger mapping of Reggie's skull. I declined, and if I was frosty about it, well who wouldn't be?

Eventually Reggie and I reconvened in my office to discuss our detective work.

"There are three approaches we could take," he began. "The most obvious one is to confront each person on the list and see if one offers up any hints of being guilty."

"No, no. That would be far too public and far too time-consuming."

"Affirmative. Besides, I did a little preliminary work, circumspect, not mentioning the cartridge or anything direct, just calling three of the guys on the list and asking how they were doing and working it around to talking about their feelings toward the company and HR and you. When I brought it up, two of the three agreed that physical violence would be appropriate. As I tried to draw them out, I started to worry that I'd just give them ideas, you know, planted a seed. Plus, there's the argument that the person who sounds off the loudest might be the least likely to walk-the-walk or cock-the-Glock or..." I waved a weary hand to indicate that I had gotten the point.

"So unless," he continued, "we could offer extended psychological counseling as a new outplacement benefit and get some sort of undercover psychologist detective to be in on it, the idea just isn't workable."

It could not possibly be true that two-thirds of the people on the list were secretly hoping for a chance to attack me, but there was no point in debating an unworkable plan so I waggled fingers to encourage him to move on.

"The next two ideas both involve a nifty little sting operation."

I sagged. "I've learned over the years that everything always comes out. Whatever we do, it has to be squeaky clean. We have to assume Mr. Cone will know about it and also be prepared for it to be made public."

Reggie gave me the hard-eye, contemplating. He conceded: "You're right—squeaky." Or did he mean it, "You're right, Squeaky"? Hmmm. I think it was the former, because he added, "We all use that old saying about someone with an ax to grind. Well, now there are more bitchy websites than there are axes, and they all love to grind away." He grinned. "The one called MundaneIndustries-Sux.com is pretty entertaining, though."

"That's one of the ones that's blocked on the office computers."

"Yeah, but the mobile version for smart phones works fine, even the photos."

That one stung, given that at this moment there was photographic evidence laying about on Genghis' desk, and before I could turn off the image, a vision of my photo being sent around via smartphone and sniggered at in every corner of the corporation made my eyes close in pain. I forced myself to stay in the moment, asking, "So what else do you have, besides the sting operations?"

"Hold on, Win. Don't give up on those yet. I was just picturing how the story of the sting operation would look in a newspaper account or HR blogs, and I'm thinking you'd come out a hero. Here you are, facing a death threat, and you devise a clever solution to trap the perp. You have a whole new image. Not quite the Toughest Sheriff in Town level of new image, but something new and manly."

"Let's hear it." I wasn't optimistic but know how to fake it.

"Two possibilities. First, we invite all the people on the list in for exit interviews. We do it in groups, for efficiency's sake, so it would come across like it was a group exit interview. We get someone from outside the company who can get the group going, get them fired up, and see from behind the one-way mirror who has *the rage*."

Not bad, I thought. That idea definitely had potential. After all, exit interviews are a reasonable thing to do. Legitimate. Evidence of a concerned HR department, working to help former employees in their transition. Okay, so maybe one of the transitions was straight to jail for the planned assassination of the SVP of HR, but we might actually learn something useful about the outplacing of employees.

I complimented Reggie on the idea, adding, "My only issue would be the budget. We'd need a moderator and facility and so on. But I think I know where I could allocate the expense. Let me think about that one."

"The other idea would solve the budget problem and would involve fewer people, which is always a good thing. What we do is a phone interview with each of them, letting them think it's a kind of job interview. We'd say that we are creating a list of potential re-hires for when business picks up. Over the phone we can get a sense of their attitudes toward the organization and, specifically, toward HR. If we pick up bad vibes, then we invite them in for an in-person follow-up where we can really dig into the nature of the animosity."

"And when you say *we*..." I switched an index finger back and forth between the two of us.

"Old habit. I meant *me*. I'd have to do the calls because I need to work your name into the conversation and see what sort of reaction I get." This was a relief, but I pretended to need convincing that I should give up my share of the calls. Then I asked myself, was the plan squeaky clean? Well, I could make the case. It would be good to have a list of potential re-hires, just in case.

That just left one obvious problem to point out: This endeavor would take a lot of time, and one thing you can say about Mundane Industries and Genghis Cone is that no one had free time. (Genghis liked to say, "There is no such thing as free time—it's just a matter of who's paying.")

Reggie suggested that someone from my department could make the contact and set up the interview times and that he'd only need five or ten minutes with each person.

"But," I wondered, "what about the people who aren't interested in talking to us about being re-hired?"

"We could use the exit interview ploy with them, keep them talking."

"I like it. I just worry, knowing how busy you are, about you taking on all that extra work." Reggie leaned back in his seat, and that's when I had a realization about him, that this was a first for him, the first time that his back had ever touched the backrest; he always leaned forward.

From a leaning distance he said, "I like the idea of saving your butt. Even more, I like the idea of you being indebted to me, Win." He did not smile.

He Died a Cheeseley

WELL, MY YOUNG NEPHEW, your mother phoned me yesterday, and we had a nice chat about you. I hope to sit down with you in person someday soon and hear about this girl you're dating, and perhaps I can attend one of your choir performances.

She tells me that you have registered for the next semester at school and that you stuck with your same old Business major, Human Resources. Though I have failed to persuade you so far, I shan't falter. If we had a family motto, it would be Carry On. (In truth, it would be, What Now? But I hope you'll join me in upgrading the family ethos.) We don't do things the easy way, we Cheeseleys. It's right there in our name, you know. It's not an easy name to live with, is it? I'm not sure if your mother ever told you this story about our name. One of our ancestors decided to take the easy way out and change his name from Cheeseley to Chessley. He wrote to tell his mother of his intention to make the change, just as soon as he returned home from his time in the military. Two days later he was killed in the battle of the Little Big Horn. He died a Cheeseley. Other ancestors took that as a warning, and it's been cheese over chess ever since. So, it's in our genes to carry on. I will persevere in my efforts to avert your career disaster.

The Cranial-Rectal Inversion

REASON #17: Human Resources conferences…
all they talk about is Human Resources.

I'VE TAKEN A COUPLE OF DAYS away from the office to attend a national HR conference, this one in San Diego. I know you've spent time in San Diego, so you may know the hotel where we held our meetings, the Marriott at the Marina. Classy place. You know it's classy when your bed is wearing a scarf—a two-foot wide strip of colorful material near the foot of the bed. All the other bedding is white-white so you don't have to wonder what's lurking in the multicolor swirl patterns that I'm guessing must be sold to lesser hotels as stain-camo.

Even in classy hotels there are lesser/cheaper rooms, of course, and befitting the representative of a company called Mundane, I was in one of those. However, if you looked past the dumpsters, there was a nice view of the wing with rooms that did have views and you could use your imagination and the reflection off all their sliding doors.

Speaking of the view, there used to be a statue by the bay showing a much larger-than-life version of the famous photograph of the sailor kissing a woman in Times Square at the end of WWII. It's gone. I asked around, and one of the other attendees told me that it was only meant to be temporary. She added, "That's a good thing." Surprised, I said I miss it and she huffed, "It's a tribute to sexual assault." Ah, the HR crowd.

I'm not presenting at this year's conference, although I have presented three other times. Two years back I presented a revolutionary idea for training departments around the country. I think you may find this interesting...

Even as I type that, I note that in my experience, nothing interesting follows the phrase "you'll find this interesting," but... well... I'll carry on...

In preparation for my program, I conducted a survey among our employees about possible new training programs. When I graciously offered them the chance to say what training topic they'd most like to see given attention in the future, the most common answer was, "A training program on how to get out of going to training programs." Cute. But that snarkiness became an inspiration to me, forcing me to realize that the managers who most needed training were the ones least likely to sign up for it.

When I talked to some weakling managers, I realized that my presuppositions had it wrong—it wasn't that they were insecure, unwilling to have their weak leadership skills exposed; no, the lousy bosses didn't turn out for training because they thought they already knew all there was to know about being a boss. The worse the boss, the higher the self-appraisal. I once heard someone describe his manager as having a "cranial-rectal inversion." Ironically, the bigger the head, the more easily it fits in; ergo, the bigger the head, the even bigger the ass-hole.

For my presentation I found some academic research by a couple of psychologists who...

Okay, okay. Never mind. I can sense your eyes glazing over—I know enough about the subject to know I know more than most people want to know.

Back to my conference presentation two years ago... what I did was devise a series of un-classes. We would try to create training designed for the very people who made the crack about getting out of training classes. We developed online training experiences, and if they watched the videos and answered a few questions about them, they could skip attendance at the classroom session.

It works so well that we were able to greatly reduce the number of classroom sessions, which saved a fortune in Danishes and bagels alone, not to mention staff hours. Genius, no?

No.

I really thought that my presentation was my ticket back to the pinnacle of my profession, making that elusive award as HR Executive of the Year a lock. Ha! It turns out that very few people who work in Training are interested in ways to eliminate people who work in Training. Leaving me to this principle...

REASON #18: Human Resources—too many humans and not enough resources.

That reminds me of one cynical colleague who confided in me this observation on business: "A penny saved by an employee is a penny earned by upper management."

As for this year's conference, I wish you'd been with me as that would do more than these journal entries to deflate your youthful soufflé of enthusiasm.

Here is a cruel twist: One of this year's speakers is Ms. Roberta Grey-Black of Wiseman & Regary. She's the woman I met at my ill-fated charity dinner, the one Carlota introduced me to shortly after my performing heroic zipper duty. She was here to make the case for outsourcing the entire HR function.

Listening to Grey-Black make her pitch, I began to think that such a scenario might not be all bad for good old Win-Win Cheeseley; after all, things would remain mostly unchanged excepting a few technicalities of payroll and legal. Then, however, during the Q&A, Grey-Black mentioned that the company sold its services to upper management by offering to reduce total employee costs. An astute questioner soon ferreted out the ugly truth: In order to reduce employee cost and at the same time make a profit for Wiseman & Regary, the solution was to cut employees' pay and benefits. Part of the implementation was a sleight-of-hand to disguise the extent of the cuts, but employees would pay a much greater share of benefits and the headcount would be pared down. So, a penny saved on employees would be half a penny earned by upper management and half a penny by W&R.

How could this possibly be advantageous to me? Well, I would remain in place, but at my current job there are no advancement opportunities. I am already Assistant to the King. But, at Wiseman & Regary, I might have a chance to move up. Because it's an HR company, being an HR person would not be the dead-end it is in other organizations. Assuming, that is, that they kept me on in my current job.

I resolved to put Roberta Grey-Black at the top of my to-be-networked agenda for the conference.

"The Void That Fills the Void"

I DON'T SUPPOSE you've come to know the rhythms of professional conferences, but they usually start the day with a big audience draw—often a paid presenter such as a former athlete—trying to motivate attendees to arrive on time, followed by a speaker on some topic considered important, then lunch, then the afternoon break-out sessions. The most popular format of these break-out sessions is the panel discussion, what the economist John Kenneth Galbraith once called, "The void that fills the void." That assessment notwithstanding, these panels are popular with both conference planners and presenters. The beauty for the presenters is that they don't have to present; rather, they merely just turn up and wing it. This makes it easy for conference planners to get commitments from executives who can't be bothered to prepare a speech and/or who don't have anything new to contribute. Plus, no one gets paid to be on a panel.

The typical panel has a moderator and four members. If you aren't familiar with breakout sessions, you might be lured into thinking this would make the session four times as interesting, but the math runs the other direction toward the law of diminishing returns. Everybody is winging but nobody is flying.

The first half of the afternoon offered up three break-outs from which to choose. The first was called "The Very Wary Eye: Learning to Spot Employee Depression." That alone might make you rethink your career choice.

However, it was not the most depressing topic of the morning—a second panel was "The Rebirth of Hope: Dealing with Suicidal Employees." I opted for the third option with the zippy name "Let's All Agree on Inclusiveness." This topic, as you'll soon see, was suicidally depressing in its own way, but the moderator was a former colleague who had called and asked me to submit an example to be discussed by the panel.

We had four panelists, three women and a man. Each was an HR executive with a major firm, which means that there is zero chance of you having heard of any of them, so I will just refer to them as Eeny, Meeny, Miny, and Mo. We were told that they would be "deconstructing" examples of "actual corporate communications." Hence the moderator's search for provocative items. Playing along, I had sent a communication that I knew would make them squeal. It was a copy of our most recent company Christmas card. Genghis himself had sent me the message that was to go inside the card, and right away I knew we had problems. I offered to edit it, delicately suggesting that I "tighten it up," only to have him respond that if I did he would tighten up my department budget. Then he told me the message was written by his granddaughter, whereupon I declared it "perfect just the way it is."

The moderator saved our card till last and held it up by a corner as if it were some sample about to be hustled off to the CDC for analysis. He described the format of the card's message, a series of "May your..." statements. The first was, "May your Santa be jolly." The moderator read it, and the audience responded with glum chuckles to suggest "How could anyone be so insensitive?" One of the panelists gave a superior smile and said, "That one is too obvious. We don't want to limit ourselves to Christmas imagery. You could solve the problem by adding Hanukkah, but even so it would be non-inclusive. We have, for instance, a number of Buddhists at our company."

Just to goad them, I raised my hand and said, "If we have some Buddhists who want to send out cards to celebrate the birth of Buddha, maybe they even call it Buddhamas, would you object?"

That notion threw the group into confusion. After all, no one wants to censor the expression of any minority. In the end, though, they were able to conclude that censoring the expression of a majority was justified. As Mo put it, "Our job is to avoid exclusion. That has to be the first goal of an inclusiveness program. Only the dominant group can make a minority groups feel excluded." Another member of the audience pointed out that this would mean that only popular ideas were excluded, and the level of rationalization reached the point where members of the Neo-Nazis were brought into it and my eyes glazed over.

While I knew Santa would be censored, I didn't anticipate the consternation caused by a granddaughter's wish "May your feet stay warm." Eeny winced at that one and said, "This is a painful one for me personally because one of my employees, a diabetic, had a foot amputated last year." To this, Meeny offered the revised statement, "May your foot/feet stay warm," but Eeny noted the likelihood that the other foot would be going soon, so the panel agreed the whole statement should be struck.

The next statement was "May your turkey be hot and juicy." This one our moderator took on personally. "I'm going to show my bias here. I am vegan…" Well, you can imagine the rest of her complaint, but I bet you couldn't imagine her solution, which was, "May your turkey/Tofurkey be hot and juicy."

Then there was "May your jokes be funny." Mo held his bald head in his hands and said, "I hate to be a killjoy, but

I have had more feelings hurt and complaints generated by lame attempts at humor than by any other type of statement. I hate to think of myself as anti-joke, but..." He shrugged and let that sentiment float out to the group and he got back sympathetic murmurs. One member of the audience tried to help, suggesting the revised line "May your expressions of humor be appropriate." Sigh.

Next, you can imagine the outrage occasioned by "May your champagne be bubbly." You'd think we were forcing every employee to chug Jack Daniels before being dragged into the driver's seat of company trucks aimed straight up the down ramp of the nearest freeway.

There was more, but once the granddaughter's sweet wishes were reduced to "appropriate humor" and "turkey/ Tofurky," you can understand how Seasons Greetings seemed miraculously just right. The inclusiveness panel had excluded just about everything.

And now you see why the depression or suicide panels might have been comparatively lighthearted.

For the afternoon session, we heard from Fig Figlar, a discount motivational speaker. I've actually hired this guy for a few of our Mundane Industries events, and well, he was a bargain. For the conference, he led us in a session on anger management. He began by having us practice anger, an assignment that gave my gentle colleagues a chance to release their pent-up rage.

REASON #19: We in HR are in the bottling business—it's our job to take anger and put it up in a pent (whatever that is).

Figlar gave us the assignment to think about the most frustrating person in our organization and to write down the ugliest, most hostile things we could possibly say to that person.

Being nasty does not come naturally to me, and my first draft was weak tea, a long whine of grievances about working for Mr. Cone. Figlar asked for volunteers to read their anger essays, and as I listened I picked up some hot ones. One of the ones I liked sounded like something from Shakespeare: "You put his brain in a thimble, and it would disappear." And there was this zinger: "He's proud of his ability to fart, and why not? It's the one thing he really excels at."

The audience got into these insults and actually cheered. Turns out, we sweet-natured HR types are a cesspool of resentments, and I could see it wouldn't take much for the group to turn into a mob carrying pitchforks and torches and setting witches on fire.

On a second draft, I got into the spirit a bit more, but the best I could do was "worse than inconsiderate, he's anti-considerate—he works at being offensive and rude."

Figlar wandered by and asked how I was doing. I showed him my work, and he encouraged me to be more vicious, suggesting for instance that I remember times that employees had mocked him.

I kept going but didn't have any real Tabasco till Figlar paired us up and I was schooled in insults by a tall woman who reminded me of Michelle Obama, although, ironically, she wasn't Afro-American. Greek ancestry, I guessed. There's something about the First Lady that makes me think she's holding in a lot of rage and would like to be the First UnLady. If so, she could take notes from my insult partner, who went on a rant, but not until after she'd asked me to take notes because she was going in "a state of truth-telling consciousness." She then described a co-worker as "a blob of pudding in human shape." She was so expressive and so animated that she started to seem like a character in a romantic comedy, the one destined to marry the man she claimed to despise. But this was real life, and she told me that she was putting in place a plan to get him fired. Given what I'd seen of her, this would probably be a preferable outcome for the guy than a romcom movie fate of marriage.

The anger management exercise wore on, and we were taught how to redirect our anger into good... blah, blah. Figlar told us that he had planned on a big finish by having us burn our anger essays in a fire pit in the courtyard, but having learned that there was a smog alert and a no-burn restriction we were instructed to take the essays home and burn them in our home fireplaces or barbecue grills. This struck me as foolishly dangerous, walking around with a document capable of not just getting you fired, but getting you forever branded with the career-death label: NOT A TEAM PLAYER. In fact, as I tucked my sheet with my mild insults and my notes from the more vicious classmates deep inside my padfolio, I realized that Fig had made a big mistake with his anger essay exercise and was going to undo someone's career. I made a friendly but scolding note on my Speaker Evaluation Sheet.

So much for detailing for you the events of the conference itself—what I've described was the most interesting part of day one. Let me say that again... the most interesting part. There were two more days of this stuff. That's what you'd be in for in HR.

On the personal side, the conference still offered me both romance and danger.

WhoaHo! It's not often that my job leads me to romance or danger. That should keep you reading.

The Women of HR

THE ROMANCE and the danger came from two different women. (If only I were able to find both in one
woman! ...*If only*... Put that on my tombstone.) Both
these women were at the conference, and so both are in
my profession.

A few words about the women of HR...

The field is predominantly female. You see different
numbers, but usually they're in the 70-80% range. I've
even met people at other companies who tell me I'm the
first male HR person they've ever met. (One young guy
said to me, goggling, "I met a male nurse when I had my
colonoscopy," like I was the second white tiger he'd laid
eyes on.) Why so female? Some of what you hear...

A. It's because women are better suited for the job. They
are more open and compassionate, more empathetic,
more nurturing.

B. More males than females are money- and status-driven.
Because HR doesn't pay as well as management or
marketing and offers fewer chances at the top jobs,
more males follow the money, and the money leads
them away from HR.

C. Because math- and science-oriented jobs are male-
dominated (Engineering, Research, Finance), corporations pack as many women as possible into fields like

HR so their gender headcounts won't make them targets for charges of discrimination. (You see the irony: They discriminate by department in the hope that it sorta balances as non-discrimination.)

Keeping this journal has given me a heightened awareness of all things HR, and after the conference dinner ended, I found myself seated with a pleasant woman from the Northwest who was willing to discuss what I've been writing you about. She's older, probably mid-fifties, with a flirty laugh and red hair, giving her a look like an older version of Christina Hendricks, the woman who plays Joan on Mad Men. Let me call her Mad Joan. She told me she needed a drink and led me to one of the hotel bars where she ordered a double Jack Daniels and soda and was asking for another before I'd downed half of my Coors Light.

I asked her view of the predominance of women in HR, easing into the topic by mentioning the theory of her gender being more compassionate and empathetic. She surprised me with this response: "Here's what it is. Women have a greater capacity to listen to whining, which, after thirty years in the field, I am starting to lose."

She gave me a look that years of listening to secrets told me meant she was deciding whether or not to press ahead and really confide in me. I gave her an out-with-it twinkle. She complied. "I shouldn't say anything. I wouldn't have even admitted that I was losing patience, but there's something about losing out on the Person of the Year Award that has made me feel a little reckless. Cheers."

Ah, that's where I'd seen her, up on stage, one of seven nominees. "We're soul mates," I responded, then told her of how I'd been swindled out of my award by the ineptitude of my regional organization.

I don't know if it was confessing my professional tragedy or the Jack Daniels, but she told me a remarkable story...

"Just last week I got this odd fantasy while listening to Marybeth in Bookkeeping accuse her manager of stealing her yogurt out of the break room refrigerator...

"Marybeth is whining on and on about this yogurt and her boss, refusing my attempts to get her onto some more important topic. Eventually I assertively interrupt and say, 'I have a magic trick. It'll make you forget all about your problems. You want to see it?'

"Naturally, Marybeth says yes, but reluctantly because she doesn't really want to forget her problems. She wants to wallow in them. Still, she has to say yes; she wants to see my magic trick. Then I carefully set a penny in the middle of my desk and say, 'I want you to examine this coin and read to me exactly what it says. Exactly.' Teary, self-righteous Marybeth stands and leans over, face inches from the coin, concentrating. That's when I put my hand on the back of her head and bounce her forehead off the desk. The penny sticks to her forehead. She screams and peels it off and there's a little Lincoln pressed into her makeup, and I say, 'See?'

"She cries out, 'See what? That hurt, you bitch!'

"And I calmly reply, 'Ah, but now the missing yogurt seems like nothing. That's... tadaaa... magic!'"

I gaped at her, as stunned as if she'd dribbled my head off a penny on the bar. She just shrugged. "Do you think I've been in this job too long?" then barked a laugh.

In the interest of research and this journal I asked, "Okay, it's an occupational hazard that you meet with too many aggrieved employees, and it can wear you down. But before, back when you were new, what would you have been thinking when listening to employee complaints?"

She thought so long I thought she'd forgotten the question, but then came up with some ripe stuff. "When I was new, I treated each issue as if it were important. I'd tell myself that if it's important to the employee, well, golly gee, it's important to me. I cared about that missing yogurt like it was an abducted child. That lasted a year or two. Then I found that my mind would wander. So I taught myself a trick, thanks to all those body language seminars."

She paused, making me insist on her coming out with it.

"If you're with an employee and you start thinking about... well, whatever... say, what you're going to do for lunch... your eyes tend to drift up, away from the person, who sometimes notices, and since they're there demanding to be listened to, you don't want them to notice that you aren't really listening. So what to do? I started amusing myself by mentally giving the person a make-over. Instead of dreaming of putting Lincoln on Marybeth's forehead, I would have been thinking of reshaping her eyebrows. So I'm really focused on her face, but not the complaint, and the time skips along."

Amazing. "I can confidently say a man would never have thought of that."

"No, a guy would be working hard not to let his eyes drift down to Marybeth's cleavage and start trying to figure out the size of her nipples."

Yikes! She'd managed to startle me once again. "This is not the sort of blunt talk I associate with the women of HR."

She scoffed. "I guess it's that I've also heard one too many harassment stories. The past few years it seems that it's all I do. I had one department of thirty-five women who were convinced their male manager kept his office at freezing temperatures because it made their nipples hard. So I had to talk to him about it. God, how I hate those conversations. His defense was, 'I have a medical condition where I sweat excessively.' Fine. But does he stop there? No. He adds, 'Besides, I'm an ass man.' What do you do with that? After all these years, you'd think guys would figure out that they have to pretend to be eunuchs. I suppose we should invent blinders like horses wear, but for corporate men. The guy-blinders would keep them from looking down."

I couldn't believe I found myself wondering, "But then they'd blunder into the dwarfs and we'd have to deal with those complaints."

"No, we'd just issue the dwarfs those skinny poles with fluorescent orange flags."

With that, Mad Joan grabbed my forearm, laughing till she snorted. You have to love a woman who laugh-snorts.

Shortly after that I mentioned you and my journal project. I told her I was trying to describe what the women in HR are like. I wanted her thoughts, but she insisted I go first.

"I'm biased, naturally, but I find the women to be especially feminine. And attractive. I don't believe there's ever been a *Playboy* profile of The Women of HR, but there could be."

She agreed. "We do get the perky ones. Bubbly. The ones who don't have another profession in mind, and so they say, 'I want to work with people.'"

She drained her glass while I urged her to tell me more, even though I sensed that she was losing interest in the topic. Still, she added, "You go into HR because you're a team player. Because you want to take care of people. So we get the kids who were on the student council and on the spirit team... whatever that is. What is that?"

"When I started seeing it on resumes, I asked around. From what I can tell, it's the people who would have been cheerleaders a couple of decades ago, when it was a combination popularity and beauty contest. Now cheerleading is gymnastics, and they're real athletes instead of being the biggest fans. We don't get many athletes in HR.

"The competitors, the fire-in-the-belly ones, want to be in sales or marketing. And we get the spirit team, the people-people, the pleasers, the peacemakers, the nicest people in town."

"Who are mostly women," I noted.

She gave me a look that I couldn't interpret. "One mark of nice men is that they actually believe women are nicer than men."

This put us within reach of the third rail. Smart men, nice or not, don't make generalizations about women. "Aren't they?"

"So you are either a genuinely nice man or wise enough to play the part. Which is it?"

Before I could answer, she added, "Tonight I could use a man who isn't *too* nice." She stood. "I'll be right back. The Ladies'."

I stood as she left, being old-fashioned. As I watched her depart, Putin swaggered up, and I was glad to see him. "Here's your chance," he told me, "to start a new rumor." He let his gaze travel over the departing figure of Mad Joan. Without enthusiasm he noted, "Better hurry. She'll be sick or asleep in thirty minutes."

I turned and saw that he was right. We both watched her pretending to be sober, using the backs of the barstools she passed as support.

Putin chuckled. "The old ones have their advantages. They don't shock. When you get her upstairs, ask her for whatever you've wanted and have not dared speak. Whatever, however. Just don't mention your mother." He slapped me on the shoulder. "Be strong. Be rhino." He stared hard into my eyes, and I noted I was just a tad taller. He gently patted my face and sighed. What had he seen in me that disappointed him? Before I could ask, he turned and was gone.

When she returned, she bluntly told me that she needed the most human of resources. We went to her room. Modesty prevents me from giving details, but I hoped Putin glanced in because I put on quite a show, and so did she. If you have a chance to bed an older woman, do not pass it by.

The Senator's Wife

I AWOKE THE NEXT MORNING—in my own room—feeling grand, plotting how I was going to turn the prior evening into gossip that would end the silly gay nonsense.

Still feeling manfully playful, when I saw my Mad Joan in line for the breakfast buffet I slipped in behind her and walked two fingers up her spine from her shoulder blades toward her neck, knowing that she loved to have her neck involved in... well, what we used to call necking.

She pulled away and spun on me, and I gave her my knowing smile, waiting for her to see that it was her lover and to melt girlish. Instead, she said, "If you've lost your name badge, I doubt you'll find it there." Distant. She was playing it cool, and I admired that.

"It wasn't just my badge that you took off me last night," I said in a near whisper.

She looked confused... or maybe it was nervousness? "I think you have me confused with someone else. Sorry."

And she turned back to the tray of frittatas.

Hmmm. There's playing it cool, and there was this, playing it cold.

Perhaps she had gone back into her HR shell, pretending to be above it all. No one was around us, so I decided to give it the all-clear. "It's okay, at least on my end. I'm not married. I don't mind a little gossip. It's even a good thing, in a way."

She doubled her concentration, moving to the Potatoes O'Brien, then slid forward to the muffins.

I pressed on. "There's this ridiculous rumor that I'm gay, and you, of all people, know it isn't true."

She placed her plate on the buffet table and turned to me. "Listen, friend, I'm not even sure who you are."

Like JFK responding to Khrushchev's letters about the Bay of Pigs, I chose to focus on the most favorable part of her response. "Yes, we are friends, and I'm so pleased to hear you call me that, even if you need to pretend not to know me, because we became great friends last night and I hope we always will be friends."

"No, I'm not your friend. Calling people friend is just a trick I learned when I started having trouble remembering names. And I hope this isn't some sort of pickup line. I'm not interested and not available. I'm flattered, but still... Now, please, let me eat my breakfast in peace. I have a bit of a headache."

"I don't doubt it. All that Jack Daniels you drank." This made her look hard at me, and I pressed on: "Don't pretend you don't know me. We met in the bar last night and you drank Jack Daniels and we talked about women in HR and you said you needed the most human of resources and we went to your room."

She went from cold to hot in that instant, from baffled to accusing. "You asshole. Are you saying that you got me drunk and I passed out and you date-raped me?"

What? How could this be? "No, not at all. I'm saying you were funny and charming, and we went to your room and you were wide awake, so awake the next room complained to the front desk and called the room. You kept singing Elvis songs. I could have the people from the front desk back me up."

"Shit. That does sound like me. Motherfuck. What song?"

"Mostly 'Blue Christmas,' which didn't seem appropriate,

but then nothing was inappropriate at that moment."

"Shit. Well, then, that means I was conscious. And it's coming back to me now. I was only drinking with you because I thought you were gay. I didn't need this. I just reconciled with my husband, and he's coming in today."

"Husband? You weren't wearing a ring. And you never mentioned a husband when you were coming on to me."

"I'm not wearing a ring because we've just reconciled, and he's bought me a new ring for our new start. He's arriving here because he's one of the main speakers, and none of this can get to him. None. Not a word of it. If it does, I'll insist you got me drunk and took advantage of me. If you tell anyone about this, I'll press charges for date rape." She saw me recoil and stepped closer. "And don't try saying it isn't true and that the charges will be thrown out because it won't matter and you know it."

Here she meant the terror of modern corporate life— get charged with any sort of sexual harassment, much less date rape, and you become a pariah. Spoiled goods. Even if upper management doubts that it's true, they have to act as if. Failure to respond is itself a charge, and everyone in HR knows it.

The smooth political Winslow stepped up and calmly said I would abide by her wishes, adding that I wanted a chance to get to know her again, like in the movies where one spouse has a head trauma and doesn't know the other. "I liked you, and we can forget about last night and just be colleagues. Just friendly colleagues."

"No. You must stay away from me. Don't even look at me. Starting now." And she snatched up her tray and turned her back and called to some woman and went to join her.

So that concludes the section I have labeled Romance, although having put it down on paper, I see that it's not terribly romantic. More sad than anything else. I am picturing you thinking, If I knew this was what the future holds, I might as well end it all. From what I can see, what the future holds is something much worse. Still you must press on, no? Just to see what it holds. Just to see.

Now for the Danger

ANYWAY... THAT WAS MY ROMANCE. Now for the danger.

If your memory is good and you've been giving this journal sufficient attention, you'll remember that Carlota introduced me to Roberta Grey-Black, with Wiseman & Regary, the Evil Empire of HR outsourcing. And you may also recall that I'd decided that having an outsider take over my department might not be all bad, assuming they kept the staff, including me. It might offer me some new upward mobility, in contrast to Mundane Industries, where I have none. This explains why I sought out this woman, wanting to start politicking.

(Most corporate employees belittle office politics. I know better. If you say "I refuse to play politics," you are playing politics. If you actually mean it, then you are playing them poorly.)

I had my eye on Grey-Black the entire conference and finally saw my chance. She was marching down the corridor alone. I say marching because she could give posture lessons to the North Korean army. Not that she's Asian. She's got perfect white-white skin, and perfect raven hair, every strand knowing its place and afraid to move, and was wearing a charcoal suit, mannish, with cuffed trousers whipping around black pumps with red soles. Everything about her announced Full Retail.

This, I told myself, was someone with whom to align myself. What a delightful change it would be to work with someone willing to spend some money after my years with Genghis and his War of the Nickels.

I nearly had to jog to fall in beside her, and I re-introduced myself, reminding her that we'd met at the charity dinner. She stopped and gave me her attention, which felt like some *Star Trek* tractor beam pulling me into her personality. I was brash, telling her that she needed to know me and that she should get started on that assignment while at the conference. She pointed to a coffee bar down the hall, and we settled into wickedly uncomfortable little chairs meant to keep tables turning.

We did the usual talk of b-schools and companies and mutual acquaintances, and I found myself liking her. She was bright and quick-witted and had a way of emphasizing a point by tapping the back of my hand resting on the tiny tabletop. So I dove in and said, "I've heard the rumors that Wiseman & Regary has been pitching Mundane Industries."

The slightest flicker, a micro emotion, told me that she was surprised that I knew.

"Mr. Cone and Carlota and I are very close," I lied, and my fingers joined in the lying when my hand went up with the middle and index fingers up in an embrace. I followed with this whopper: "Naturally, they want my input. I can't decide how to feel about the plan."

She was smart enough to know that this was political arabesque, offering a possible coalition. She bit. "Most HR execs fight us. They lose, but then they win. They don't realize that working with us has many advantages, especially for the person in charge. It's the end of loneliness."

I urged her to tell me more.

"Problems rise up the organization, and the nastier the problem, the faster it rises. Right to the head of HR. And then you have to decide whether or not to take it out of HR and to the President or Executive Committee. If you're like most concerned HR execs, you spend a lot of time deliberating what you can say to whom. But if you're part of W&R, you have people to talk to. You're no longer alone."

That sounded good, and before our coffee was finished, she'd gone on to also dangle career advancement. I must have impressed her, I thought, because she told me the story of one of their Regional Presidents who'd come from a company the size of mine and who'd had three promotions and now oversaw HR in 17 companies and used a company jet to visit them.

(Genghis had once announced to his team that he had acquired a company jet for all of us to use. We were stunned and then thrilled. Just for an instant we all were James Bond, drinking a martini on the way to Manhattan. Then he pulled a toy plane out of his briefcase. "Here it is. If anyone needs the company plane, just stop by my office and borrow it." We applauded his joke, all bravo-bravo, but I know everyone felt as I did, that our guardian angels had dozed off the day we joined Mundane Industries.)

Roberta Grey-Black gave me a little hug before she left me, and I felt that this was the start of something good.

That feeling lasted three minutes. I was staring at my watch, deciding whether or not to attend the panel discussion on better panel discussions, when I spotted Mad Joan seated across the coffee shop. I recalled her threats and went to turn away, but she stood and waved. I saw then that she was seated with a Senator, and that's when I recalled that he was to be the keynote speaker. Then it all clicked. He was to be the speaker and he'd just flown in and was meeting her. This was her husband. Somehow this made our liaison the previous night seem dirty. But in a good way.

From a dozen paces away I could see the wedding ring rainbowing as she passed under the spotlights. I pretended to be absorbed by my cellphone as I monitored her movements with my peripheral vision, debating with myself as to whether I hoped she was coming to speak to me or hoped she would pass me by.

She sat in the seat Grey-Black had just vacated. Despite her friendly wave, I acted like I couldn't quite place her, letting her know I would play the stranger.

"It's okay. You don't have to pretend you don't know me. I told my husband you were a gay guy that I met last night." I looked over, and he waved merrily and a bit swishily while talking on his phone.

"And last night came back to me, sort of. You were sweet. And now we'll forget last night happened. Agreed?"

"Didn't happen." Feeling mischievous I stretched and added, "I'm a little sore in the lower regions, but that must be from the escalators being out."

"Don't be naughty. I didn't come over here because of that. I came over here because I saw you with Roberta Grey-Black."

"Isn't she great? I think I may end up working for her company."

She shook that off with an exaggerated shudder. "You poor ignorant child. She's the devil. You must get a wooden cross and drive it through her heart."

She explained that she'd been in two different companies where W&R had come in to take over HR. Both times she'd been hired by Roberta Grey-Black, given a new agreement with benefits slashed, and then, within months, axed via layoff, with a pitiful severance package because, as she was told at the time, she was just a "new" employee.

"The second time it happened, four years ago, I'd been in my same office, same desk, for eleven years, but I was a new employee and given one month of salary as severance."

"But they need people. They offer a career ladder."

"Did she tell you about the company jet?"

I blanched.

"Me too. I thought I'd be a star with them. But instead of moving people up, they move them out. They have all the detail work done in India and so they cut the staff at the companies they sign up. They mostly cut the expensive people. So it's great if you've got three or five years in and you get promoted to manager; you get paid half of what you or I would get but you think you've fallen into whipped cream."

She could see I didn't want to believe it.

"Think about it. They offer to cut the HR expense by ten or twenty percent, plus they are making a profit. That money has to come from somewhere."

Her husband came over and gave me the grin-and-grip, squeezing my upper arm as he squashed my hand. "My wife has been telling me about you. Very impressive. I'd love to make use of your talents for the good of the country. I think you would be just right for our LBGT steering committee. Just say yes, make sure you exchange contact info with my wife, and I'll make it happen."

So much for my new image as Mr. Super-hetero.

The Kiss of Corporate Death

REASON #20: Returning.

YOU LEAVE FOR A FEW DAYS and your office fills with problems like vagrants finding an empty store's façade to piss in. When you work in HR and you're out, it's not like an assembly line where a replacement employee takes your spot, or like a classroom with a substitute teacher; no, your work just accumulates, and it accumulates faster than normal because a person who's out is defenseless— there's no way to attach a deflector shield to your desk.

Let me back up and say that work-dumping is an important corporate skill for everyone, not just those of us in HR. It's the nature of organizations in the New Economy to have everyone overworked. Work is overwork. Every employee would need an extra, oh, let's say, fifty hours a week to catch up. If you actually put in those fifty hours and caught up, then you'd attract additional work, and the next month you'd be a hundred hours behind. (I don't suppose the folks who came up with the Law of Attraction had that in mind, but it's inevitable—the Clydesdale ends up hitched to the heaviest wagon.)

Once you realize that you're never going to be caught up, then you have to make a decision. You can rail against it and attempt to refuse work and thus be thought of as a whiner and, worst of all, NATP (Not A Team Player, the kiss of corporate death). Or, you can say Sure! No Problem! to everything and become skilled at work-dumping.

The work-dumping happens to you when you're out for any reason, personal or professional. You come back and find that coworkers have given you assignments that were given to them. If they are smart, they leave a note with a bit of flattery, something like...

I talked with X and Y, and they thought you'd be perfect for this.

or

I started this then realized that it really needed your input.

or

This is right up you alley.

or

You're the expert on this.

After that, odds are they'll add a smiley face. That's a drawing of their grinning face, not yours. If they drew your face, it would have a little knife in your eyeball.

Writing such notes takes less than a minute, and they have offloaded hours of work. Okay, there the work is, on your desk. Now you need to decide where you can dump it.

Notice that in all of this the project doesn't get started or finished; thus, it's not really alive but not dead, either. That makes it a "vampire project" or a "zombie project." Both are projects that just won't die, and the terms are used interchangeably, although purists insist that a zombie is something that was dead and came back to life. These are also sometimes referred to as "a Glenn Close," after a terrific movie before your time. Ask your mom.

The current record here for a zombie project is one that was first considered and "put on the back burner" in 1993 and has yet to be completed. 1993? There's the back burner and then there's 1993, which is the can of Sterno smoldering in the alley.

In my own case, the amount of work I have is triple what it should be. I'm like the last overhead bin on a full flight, the one where they turn and stuff and punch till everything inside the carry-ons is ground to tiny particles. That's because two of my staff of four are on leave. There's Lila, my most capable employee, a tall elegant Jewish woman who has told the same joke at least once a week, for years now...

What's a Jewish nymphomaniac?
Twice a year.

Was she describing herself? Perhaps. Still, she's on maternity leave. Her doctor insists that she must spend the final trimester in bed or risk losing the baby.

Her assistant, Veronica, an intern we hired on full-time a year ago, is also out on maternity leave, although there was never any talk of additional time off as her husband is a poet and she is perpetually worried about money.

We in HR are schooled at not being sexist, but I have to tell you that maternity leave is a planning nightmare. Virtually all pregnant employees say that they are taking just a month (or two or three) and will return, but we know that a large percentage don't. Some have confided that they don't really plan to return, but want to keep the option open, just in case they go crazy staying at home or their husband loses his job or insurance or whatever. It's a nervous economy; who can blame them?

So when you have someone go out on leave, you do the work yourself or you hire a temporary replacement. Sometimes it's both. The politically savvy mom-to-be will offer to find you a replacement, then make sure they sign on a drooler, someone so dense that it's easier to just do everything yourself then explain and re-explain. Thus that shrewd pregnant employee makes sure you long for her to return. Otherwise, it can happen that the replacement is so hardworking and efficient that you're disappointed when the leave is up. I once had it happen that I said goodbye to a fabulously productive replacement employee only to have the returning new mom change her mind a month later and quit. When I called the replacement, she'd taken a full-time position the day before. I wanted to wail like a newborn.

The upshot is that I have two of my staff of five (four plus me) out. That leaves me with just Kyle, AKA FullOf-Himself, and Eileen, a grumpy woman by HR standards, but perhaps that's what makes her so efficient at handling the endless questions and complaints about her specialty: Benefits. I also have a substitute employee that Lila picked to take her place, a scrawny, snide woman who spends a lot of rubbing sanitizing lotion into her hands, a modern Lady MacBeth. Unlike the Lady, who could really get things done, this woman spends all her non-sanitizing time feverously planning her work, boasting that she's "a perfectionist's perfectionist," which makes me think of someone trapped inside an Escher drawing, furiously running up the stairs.

My substitute employee was pleased to see me return to the office, not due to my charms or talents, but because she refused to make a decision and instead waited for my return to carefully lay out the options. However, I shooed her away once I saw on my desk a handwritten note from Reggie. "Call me the minute you get back."

He informed me that he was making progress against his preliminary list of suspects for the case of the mystery bullet. (I know, I know—it was a *cartridge*. Still, it's the bullet that's the scary part.)

He'd followed our plan and was making calls to former employees, creating the so-called "rehire" list. Of dozens of calls, he'd found three men who said they'd never return to Mundane Industries and one who went so far as to say that Winslow Cheeseley was one of the reasons, underlining that assertion with enough emotion to make Reggie suspicious. He'd also talked to two others who agreed to be on the list but whose bitterness was so intense that he decided to include them in our group.

"One thing was bothering me," he said. "I was picturing these five guys in a room together, and what was wrong with that picture? No women. They would have to notice that. So I included a couple of females, including one who could conceivably be a suspect: Vanessa Truman. She had a bit of the Angela Davis in her. Remember Angela Davis?"

Yes. "Back in college I had actually heard her give a lecture, and we were all disappointed that she never mentioned the Black Panther Party or that she was tried for kidnapping and murder." Reggie looked impressed so I added, "She ended up teaching at one of the University of California schools... I forget which one. But I do remember that she was in a department called History of Consciousness."

Reggie sighed. "Christ. History of Consciousness? What's next? I bet they actually have a History of Masturbation department, and if they do the endowed chair would..."

I jumped in before he could complete that thought and asked him to tell me more about his plans for our suspects.

"Just what we talked about. I have them coming in for a group interview, like a focus group. They think they're there to help us better understand what laid-off employees go through and how we might do a better job in future lay-offs. I got us a room at the Curious Cat Research facility in Tempe. It has a one-way mirror so you can sit back and watch. And I decided I'd just lead the discussion myself. It'll save money—they offered me a moderator for five grand, the bandits, but screw that—and I'll be able to guide the conversation better than some moderator.

I did plenty of group interrogations in Nam. Those were just like a focus group... although they were prisoners and blindfolded and we knocked them around, but you know, basically the same."

I struggled to come up with a polite response.

"This will probably require a different skill set," I said cautiously.

"Come on, Win. I was joking. Relax. Just plan to be there early. No one can see you arrive."

Behind the One-Way Mirror

I ARRIVED AN HOUR EARLY and still spotted two former employees already waiting outside the research company. I'd been to Curious Cat before and so I knew there was a back entrance and I slipped in without being noticed.

I don't know if you've attended focus groups as an observer, seated behind the one-way mirror. The research facility always makes these back rooms nice because that's where the paying customers sit. There are nicely padded chairs, often in two or three raised rows like a movie house. Usually you find elaborate hors d'oeuvres and beverages, often a full bar, but this was a budget project so the refreshments were just bottled water (store brand) and a sad little tub of cheesy dip attended by a circle of crackers, which might have been off-brand Ritz; I couldn't tell because it was dark back there for the sake of the one-way mirror which requires a disparity in light to work effectively.

I took my seat and saw Reggie enter alone on the other side, squinting in the bright lights. He looked relaxed. Too relaxed. He sat at the head of the big table and lay back as if sunbathing. Then he jerked forward and began to set out colored index cards. He smiled at one card and talked to it. The microphones hadn't been turned on yet so I couldn't make out what he was saying, but clearly he had found a friend in something he saw there in one of the cards.

The door in the group room opened and the sugary young woman assigned to our project by the research facility said something to Reggie that must have included my arrival because they both looked at the mirror and waved. I waved back. Useless of course, but politeness is a habit or it is nothing.

Reggie stood, left the bright interview room and made his way around the corner to my dark little observatory. He mumbled something unintelligible, which was way out of character for a forceful personality like his. "You don't seem yourself," I ventured.

"I'm not. This girl I'm seeing gave me this pill to relax me, and it's like I smoked a dozen joints."

"Why did she feel the need to relax you? I'd think you'd want to be razor sharp for this assignment."

He tried to glare at me but gave up and sighed. "I'm going to tell you something you must never repeat. Never."

"Give me a Bible, and I'll swear."

"I'm asking you as an offi... as a gentleman. And a friend."

I hate being entrusted with secrets but I needed to hear him and so swore my oath of silence.

With self-loathing he said, "I have a thing about speaking in public."

This was a relief. As secrets go, this was up there with not liking Brussel sprouts. It was also a weakness that I'd encountered dozens of times. You'd be surprised how many powerful execs weasel out of speeches, and how many others resort to reading from a Teleprompter. When I plan meetings I sometimes have a fearsome spotlight aimed at the lectern so that my executive speaker can't see the audience and freeze. "You and everyone else. But no one's expecting a speech from you tonight. Seven people in a room, just, you know, conversing."

He wouldn't meet my eyes when he replied. "Yeah. Except they're all looking at me to start the thing, and

I was afraid I'd go blank. So I made notes but I was still twitchy enough that Mandy gave me a pill. Tiny little thing but, whoa, did it relax me."

"So everything is good. Right? The worst that can happen is that you fall asleep."

"I might barf."

"No. You aren't going to barf," I said firmly. To think of barfing is to barf, as someone wise, perhaps Descartes, once pointed out.

"Here's a trick I learned from a guy who was terrified of public speaking but went on to become a professional speaker. He began his career doing seminars and he was so nervous that he'd always start by handing something out. He'd work his way to the back of the room, handing out some summary sheet or outline. That way he was in the back and everyone was looking down and he could begin and build some momentum before he had to go up front and have everyone staring at him."

"But look," he whined and pointed out the mirror. "The people will be in a circle. No back of the room."

I wanted to slap him but said, "Just hand something out. If nothing else, give them blank paper and pencils to take notes with. They'll look at those, and you'll be fine."

I reached up and squeezed his bony, hard shoulder. "You'll make the whistle," I told him gravely. The whistle business is, I've been told, a rodeo expression meaning to stay on the bull or bronco for the required eight seconds.

I was ready to explain the reference, but he nodded and said, "I'm just joking about the speaking stuff." This was bravado, embarrassed that he'd confessed. "But not about that pill. Whoff!"

All seven attendees soon showed up and were shown into the focus group room. Reggie handed out note pads and talked hesitantly while they passed them around.

Then he handed out blue cards. Then pink cards. Then yellow ones. The whole time he stood behind the circle of former employees, speaking to heads looking down, explaining to them why they were there and what he had planned. Eventually his old manliness returned, and by the yellow cards he was joking around, although in an oddly hollow and slow voice. However, no one seemed distracted by it, so we'd passed the first hurdle.

One of his first topics, at my insistence, was to remind them that this was not an official Mundane Industries function. Our cover story was that they were volunteers in a project Reggie was doing on the side. This arrangement, he explained, gave him more freedom and leeway and they should feel the same openness, with everything "off the record."

He said that as I sat guiltily in the dark next to the camera recording the proceeding. I reached over and turned it off and felt a bit better about myself.

Why had I insisted on this disclaimer about it not being a company project? I was covering my ass and the company's too. That's what we do in HR.

REASON #21: You cover so much ass you start to feel like a box of paper toilet-seat protectors.

Reggie and I had agreed in advance that he would ease into the discussion by asking each of our seven participants-suspects to tell the group why he or she had left the company. We hoped that this would get them to open up, calling forth a feeling of kinship that might rise into a confessional camaraderie. It ended up being a fascinating exercise for me to hear, allowing me to contrast their personal accounts to what I knew from their managers. This employment version of *Rashomon* has useful lessons so I'll summarize each of the seven, employee perception versus management's explanation.

Given that these are seven strangers to you, I'll do what I did with Mad Joan and pick a famous person who most resembles each of them and I'll use that name so you can have a mental picture.

1. The first to volunteer to tell his story was a guy who is also the easier to associate with a celebrity because he'd already done it for us. He plays up a hint of a young Clint Eastwood, squinting and dressing like a cowboy. Our Clint, however, often joked about being the world's only Jewish cowboy and calls himself Clint Eaststein. I'd gotten to know him and liked having him at the company, admiring his passion and his standards. His boss, however, considered him a know-it-all and grew tired of arguing with him over how things would be done. So, when a layoff came around, Eaststein got tossed.

However, here is how Eaststein explained being let go: "My manager was jealous of me. He knew I could do his job better than he could and decided that he better get rid of me before upper management woke up and discovered they'd had the wrong guy in the job."

Sitting there, behind the mirror, I sighed. This was a common rationale. Those who've been laid off often grab hold of some version of "I was just *too good*."

2. The next ex- to speak was a light-skinned Afro-American woman who, when we both were attending a conference, described herself to me over Mai Tais as having "a JLo booty." I've since heard this several times from other women and can now conclude that this comparison to Jennifer Lopez is how big-butt women have learned to accept their bodies, rather like how bald men are forever comparing themselves to Sean Connery. In the case of the woman before me now, Jennifer Lopez could comfortably sit on her lap, and there'd still be room for a couple of large cats or small children. In other words, she could be JLo's Barcolounger, so let's call her JBarcoLo.

When it was JBarcoLo's turn to explain her being laid off, she snorted and said, "Look at me. Just look." We all did and all felt her anger scorching our eyeballs as we tried to ascertain just what part of her had caused her downfall. That mystery was cleared up when she added, "When times get tough, it's women and people of color who are the first to go."

The only other woman in the room seemed half-open to that notion, but JBarcoLo's discrimination argument was a tough sell on the rest of the group, all males who'd shared her unhappy fate.

(I have to interrupt myself here. I am sensitive on the issue of discrimination and feel the need to say that I have statistics showing that Mundane Industries has an over-representation of women and minorities as employees, whereas the layoffs had been predominately white males. Not because they were white males, but because they had tended to be in the middle management positions, and as any middle-age person of any color could tell you, fat tends to collect around the middle.

The reason we have so many women and minorities is that Mundane Industries, and our founder, Gerald "Genghis" Cone, actively uses discrimination as a hiring strategy— other people's discrimination. And it's not just minorities or women—it's ugly people or fat people, smokers or ex-cons— they are welcome at M.I. That is, they're welcome IF that discrimination has made them a bargain. We could have a statue of Mr. Cone dressed as the Statue of Liberty outside our corporate headquarters...

Give me your unselected,
Your thank-you-for-your-application-buts,
Your talented unemployables yearning for a chance,
The wretched leftovers after you've chosen up teams,
Send these, the desperate ones to me—
I lift my lamp and wave small checks.)

Getting back to our group and to JBarcoLo, I can tell you that race had indeed played a part in her being laid off, just not the way she assumed. She was the sort who took offense at everything, suspecting everyone of being racist, especially anyone who claimed not to be racist. As a white male, I've learned never to express any opinions on race, but I will tell you that accusing everyone around you of being racist is not an effective means of building alliances. No one fought to keep her when it was time to thin the herd.

3. Next was a former analyst in Market Research, whose part should be played by Joe Pesci, although our version had a much deeper voice so I'll call him Basso Pesci. He'd gotten himself thrown into the layoff pool by overspending on research projects. That wouldn't have been enough to draw more than a reprimand, but once again, he didn't have the internal support to save him when the accounting daggers got drawn. In his case, he tended to use statistics as a weapon. He had a habit of saying, "These are the facts" as a preface to a reel of numbers. Many of these were taken out of context and stretched to fit, making them part fact and part speculation—what some came to call "factulation." That led to his nickname, Factulence.

When invited to explain his departure to Reggie's group, I chuckled when he began, "These are the facts…" He'd actually compiled statistics on how often he'd been right in predicting the success or failure of products and advertising campaigns. His conclusion? "I was fired for being right."

The others in the room added a dark, grumbling assent, and Eaststein leaned over and squeezed Basso Pesci's shoulder, muttering "Fuck 'em." Here was the first glimpse of the anger waiting below the surface.

4. The mood was lightened, however, by the next one to explain her situation, a young woman who might have been played by Tina Fey, one of those beautiful women who talks about herself as a nerd who's envious of beautiful women, making me wonder if she really believes that or has simply realized it's an effective way to get people to notice her attractiveness while still thinking of her as one of the guys. Our version of Tina is 5'10", so let's call her Tall Tina. She worked for me briefly, before being noticed by Genghis, who decided he needed a new assistant. (If you've been paying attention, you'll remember that this was the same pattern we saw with my enchantress, Eve.) This sudden interest from above would be, as it had for others, her downfall. Genghis gave her a large raise, befitting her new status as reporting directly to the CEO. Over the next year, he gave her two more raises. Her work was first-rate; no one ever questioned her talent or commitment. On the other hand, everyone questioned our CEO's motives. After all, she was the only one in the company to get three raises in one year. But after that glorious three-fer of a year, Genghis tossed her onto the layoff slag pile. He came to me, her former boss, explaining that he wanted to set a good example by including someone from his staff in the layoff. He urged me to take her back into my department. However, I had budget problems of my own and told Genghis I couldn't swing it. I never did learn why he made his decision—was he tired of sleeping with her or of not sleeping with her, or was it something else altogether?

Whatever the reason, Tall Tina was one that I hated to see leave, given her energy, her eagerness to help the team and her great potential.

You can imagine my surprise when, asked to explain her departure to Reggie and the group, her sunny nature disappeared to be replaced by bitterness. "It was Cheeseley in Human Resources. I worked for him before Mr. Cone asked me to be part of his apprenticeship program. Then, when it was time to go back to my old job, Winslow Cheeseley screwed me and wouldn't take me. He did it all behind my back, too. He never had the guts to talk to me."

Eaststein muttered "Shitheel," and Basso Pesci, "He is the worst."

I yearned to pound on the glass and cry out my innocence, but all I could do was moodily bite off a piece of Ritz-ish cracker while fighting back the sense that this whole focus group project had been a mistake.

Speaking of mistakes, my descriptions are dragging on a bit, so let me get through the last few quickly...

5. The next was an older guy who might have been played by Liam Neeson, if Liam had stopped working out in 1995. Our Lumpy Liam was a salesman who'd made almost no sales. He spent his days listening to inspirational podcasts then doing visualizations of himself as a super salesperson.

"There is no training in the company," he complained to the group. "When I called them on it, they assigned me to work with that Cheeseley idiot, but he had nothing to offer. It was a case of being thrown in the shark tank and sink or swim. Tell me, do I look like I'm a great swimmer? No. But I can sell like crazy, given the chance." He slapped the table and repeated, "Given the chance."

6. Next was a Hispanic who was sufficiently fit and handsome to be thought of as our Rafa Nadal... you know, the Spanish tennis player. He was sent away for the most boring of reasons—that he was a recent hire and they had to cut someone from the department. When asked why he's been included in the layoff, he surprised me by saying, "They must have found out that I had another job and did a lot of it on the company computer. But that's so unfair because I still did more work than anyone else." News to me, and I'm sure it would be news to his manager who would have loved to have some justification for his decision.

7. Last there was a cocksure guy who reminded me of a bald David Letterman. He had a habit of pointing at you when he talked and, while he never told you anything useful or interesting, he always finished his pronouncements with "You see?" whereupon he'd drop his head and raise his eyebrows while turning the pointing finger upward as if it were an exclamation point. He was chosen for the layoff partly because he often left work early and took many sick days but mostly because, when he was there, he didn't contribute. When called upon to explain his departure, he said, "Pure politics. I backed the wrong candidate for VP, and when she got passed over, I was an innocent bystander."

The woman he was speaking of hadn't, in fact, been passed over for promotion. She'd turned it down because she has four young kids and didn't want the extra travel. Moreover, she was the one who'd chosen him for the layoff.

So there it was, seven people who'd been told to leave. Not one of them understood management's real reason. And why was that? Some might say that it was their

managers' natural human tendency to avoid conflict, or
perhaps a manager's need to be nice and not offend the
poor person being sent away. Maybe that's a part of it,
but we in HR made sure that those difficult conversations
never took place. We would instruct the managers to say
nothing about why any given employee was included in
the layoff. That means employees never get to hear the
truth and are left to concoct some story to explain it to
themselves and to their families.

You might be thinking, "That's not fair!" I sometimes
think that myself. But one of our most important jobs in
HR is to avoid employee lawsuits, and if you give reasons
for firings or layoffs those can be turned against you. But,
even ignoring lawsuits, when you pull someone aside and
give them the hard truth, they argue with you, or worse
yet, they beg and plead and promise to change. All that
messiness and emotion is avoided if you simply say, "It's
a layoff and we had to cut positions and yours was one of
them." You pretend it isn't about them. "It's just business."

**REASON #22: We may lead Training but we don't
teach our failed employees the most important
lesson of all—why they failed.**

As unpleasant as it was to be sitting there biting my
tongue, or rather, soft crackers, being forced to listen to
those ugly things being said about the company and even
about one Winslow Cheeseley, the conversation was about
to turn far more troubling.

A Really Bad Cruise Ship

REGGIE HAD TRIUMPHED over his diffidence, but now was charging over to the other extreme, starting to make cracks about the company's history of layoffs. He then asked a little Zippo of a question, "How would you grade the company's handling of your personal layoff, from A to F?"

They went around the table with the first three grades being F, F, and F. The first D, given by Tall Tina, caused Reggie to draw back, looking fogged, blurted, "Not an F?" Some ally.

"No. It could have been worse. At least they didn't hand me an empty box and tell me to pack up my personal belonging while some goon from Security looked over my shoulder."

Hmmm. Who'd let that happen? Someone had violated our strict guidelines on exiting employees. I'd been out of town when Genghis had made his decision on tossing out this talented young woman. Perhaps he waited till then, knowing I was aware of her talents and his reckless raising of her salary and had been embarrassed. If so, that would be a first.

Thinking back, I remembered that Genghis had pressed FullOfHimself to do the actual firing, immediately, rather than following protocol and waiting for me to return from my trip.

As for the empty box, the anti-gift, I was aware that it was the focus of much resentment. People hate it, and I don't blame them. But the box is part of our policy, administered by my department. In my defense, I should point out that dismissed employees left to wander about for two weeks or even a day have a record of despicable behavior—they steal client lists, they go around persuading other employees to quit, they delete important computer files, or at the extreme, attack executives or attempt suicide. Or, in one horrid case, early in my career, one took a shit on my desk. I wasn't there when the event happened, but still, imagine finding a stinking pile—it must have been All You Can Eat day at the burrito bar—waiting for you. So I accept the charges of dehumanization that come with handing an employee an empty box. Call me hardhearted but that's what the world does to the sensitive young man of HR.

REASON #23: Being the provider of the empty box, the anti-gift, the symbol of the hollow relationship between company and employee.

The other grade of D, in case you're wondering, was because I had offered to write a letter of recommendation for Clint Eaststein. Any uptick of spirits that might have come with that relatively high grade of D were dispelled when he said, "But I'd still like to rip open his chest and see if he actually has a heart in there."

I hadn't written the letter of recommendation, just made the offer, but I wished I had so I could now tear it up. Such was my impassioned state of mind that the act of tearing became so real to me that I found myself crumbling a handful of crackers, a massive mistake when wearing a fawn-colored suit susceptible to grease stains.

Reggie, now over-stimulated, further inflamed the situation by asking the employees how the layoff could have been handled better. Naturally they wanted massive severance pay and outplacement services. Sitting there, feeling misunderstood, I scoffed, saying half aloud, "If the company had the budget for all that, we wouldn't have been having layoffs."

Even as I said it I realized it wasn't true. The truth was that regular layoffs were a quick and easy way to get rid of mediocre or overpaid employees. You didn't have to build a case, just announce a lay-off and it was "You, you, and you." Brutal, but that was how the world works, which meant it was *natural*, right?

I was shaken from these Darwinian reflections by Reggie asking the group whether they had given any thought to "getting back at the company."

"Here are the facts," said Basso Pesci, the market research guy, "wrongful termination suits are just urban legend. A lawyer has to represent someone who's out of work, and someone out of work doesn't have any money, so the attorneys have to do it on spec and work for a cut of the settlement. Some of them might take that deal, but the corporations have learned to stretch it out. Years. So the lawyer has to do all that work for all that time without any guarantee of getting paid anything."

"I checked into it too," said JBarcoLo. "I went to a guy who got some money for a friend of my husband. All he did was write a letter saying he was going to file a discrimination suit for millions. Then he got the employer to settle the case for like twenty grand. The company paid the money figuring it was cheaper than paying the lawyers and that way they didn't risk having it go public that they were racists."

The entire group perked up. Bald Letterman was first to ask, "So did it work? I want that guy's name. What percentage did he take?"

She passed over him with a slow gaze of small pity that somehow managed to remind him and everyone else that he did not present a danger for bad publicity. No exec would lie awake fearing the headline: Lawsuit Alleges Company Discriminates Against Middle-Aged White Guys.

She said, "No, it didn't work. He turned me down."

"Why?" everyone asked at once.

"Because it's frigging Mundane Industries. As soon as I told him where I'd worked, he lost interest. They have a reputation of fighting every claim." This was true and something that Genghis had learned long before I joined the company. He told me "You pay 'go away' money, and it's like feeding a pigeon so it will stop hanging around and shitting on everything." (It's a corollary to his principle I mentioned earlier, "If you always say no, they'll stop asking.")

The group fell silent, each one mourning the twenty grand they'd just seen floating before their eyes. Reggie brought them back to the topic of revenge, inflaming them with, "Isn't there anything that can be done?" and "Does everyone just have to bend over and take it?"

Our Tina Fey suggested starting a support group. "We have a core right here. If we each contacted the others we know who got laid off, we could meet and try to help one another." She nodded as she spoke, pumping for enthusiasm but coming up dry.

"Sounds like a pity party to me," said JBarcoLo.

"No, it would be networking. We could spot jobs. Figure out who's hiring. Maybe we could pool our talent and go into competition with Mundane."

This set off a daisy chain of covert glances and pinched appraisals. What I knew, having talked to hundreds of departing employees, is that each one felt some version of, "I understand why the company would be laying off all these *other people*, but I'm different. *My* being in this group of losers is a big mistake."

A few offered vague support, and Reggie jumped in, saying that at the end everyone could exchange emails and get together again. Good work, I thought. Then he gave them a fierce look and dragged the group into dangerous territory, "Let's be honest with each other. I think it's only natural to think about revenge. Can we be real here?"

Bald Letterman pointed a finger at Reggie and said, "As I tell myself every morning, the best revenge is living well."

"Good attitude. But I'm talking about getting in touch with your anger."

"You've got to channel it," offered our Liam. "I like to think about getting a job with one of M.I.C.'s competitors and helping put them out of business."

Reggie pushed them but found no current of violence. Eaststein finally took the bait and said, "There is something to be said for violence. A decade or more ago they had all those freeway shootings in Los Angeles. I was living over there at the time. Before the shootings, people were always cutting you off in traffic and flipping you off. After the freeway shootings, people were like 'Oh, please, you first. No, no, please, you go ahead of me.' It's what's known as an attitude adjustment. If only someone would take out some of these executives who go around laying people off, I think they might just be a little more cautious."

I expected the group to be shocked and to turn on him, but they looked with awe, saying "Yes, yes" and Basso Pesci gave him a "That's a fact!"

Someone asked jokingly (at least I told myself it was a joke), "How many dead executives would it take?"

I tried to remember the goal of my being there and I studied each of their faces and their body language, trying to deduce who might actually act on this plot. I could only exclude our young version of Rafa Nadal and our bittersweet version of Tina Fey.

I was so preoccupied with assessing the potential for violence that I almost missed Reggie shifting the focus, asking how Human Resources fit into the picture, leading the witnesses with this outrageous question, "How much blame should we place on HR?"

The young Hispanic, our Rafa, offered an out. "My uncle is an executive, and he tells me that I should cooperate with HR but not pay them a lot of attention because the truth is that they don't have any real power."

Good boy, I thought. We may understand the value of the occasional layoff, but they certainly aren't our decision, not our call.

The group might have bought that argument, but Liam offered a more sinister interpretation. "Your uncle is right—they don't have the power of a CEO, but they do have the CEO's ear. They are the ones who should be influencing the owners and executives."

JBarcoLo snorted. "They act like allies. Like friends. But it's like the time I had to meet with an IRS agent because of my jerk ex-husband. That dude was so friendly I had to keep reminding myself that this is no way a friend of mine. No way."

"You mean," our Rafa added, "they are like a car salesman who's all, 'Let me go present this to my manager and see if I can sell it.' Like he's on your side."

So there it was, a new low, comparisons to IRS agents and car salesmen. Could it get any worse? Wait.

Liam leaned in to grimly lecture the group. "Here's what makes it 'specially bad with the creeps in HR. They are the first ones you spend time with. They have those welcome sessions for new employees and their classes and manuals. Then, they are the ones putting on the social events and handing out mugs and gift cards."

"Gift cards?" Rafa squeeked, amazed.

"Well, up till a year or two ago. Now all we get are certificates of appreciation, and those aren't even sent over to the graphics department, just some HR intern playing with Photoshop. But my point is that these are the people who indoctrinate you and put out the stuff with the company logo and come up with events. So what does that make them like?"

"A really bad cruise ship?" said Tall Tina.

Liam ignored that and slapped the conference table to refocus the conversation on him. "Like the Church. They are like Catholic priests. And so when they turn around and screw you, it's just like those rotten priests with the altar boys. That's why I say HR should be singled out for being the lowest scum."

See? Makes a comparison to car salesmen seem like a compliment, no?

Meanwhile, I could see loathing come into the eyes of several of the people in the focus group room.

Reggie chose to test their emotions by inventing a story. "I heard about a case, outside of Dallas, where a group of employees who'd been laid off actually attacked the head of the HR department."

The reactions were so fast they were virtually simultaneous, and so it was hard to recall who said what.

"I can see that"

"No shit."

"Makes sense."

There I sat, my face a foot or so from my side of the one-way mirror, and I started to believe that if the others knew I was so close they might toss a chair through the glass and drag me out over the shards.

I could see that Reggie would have to do some righteous work to cool off these seven before sending them on their way. Instead, he asked them for suggestions of how to seek revenge against HR and, specifically, against one Winslow Cheeseley. Sure, I'd agreed in our planning meeting that during the evening he would have to test the group's appetite for violence, but still it came as a shock to hear myself being thrown to this wolfpack. I wanted to cover my ears but instead pulled out my phone and sent him a text message. (We'd pre-arranged that I would send him suggestions if something came up I really wanted him to pursue.) I tapped in "Change subject!"

Even from where I was I could see his phone light up and dance a bit to the silent-mode vibrations. He ignored it for an instant, as if unwilling to miss a single word of Basso Pesci volunteering to slash my tires, then read my words without reaction. He texted back "to what?"

Electronically I shouted back, "ANYTHING! JUST CHANGE!"

Reggie shook his head a fraction of an inch in each direction and glanced my way, letting me see the disappointment in his eyes. But, a good soldier, he cleared his throat and said, "I'd like to change things up a bit. While we're talking about Cheeseley, maybe you guys can help me out. Just curious. Do you think he's gay?"

The weasel. I grabbed my phone back up to shoot another text, but held back. I confess, I was curious.

Our Letterman shook a finger and said, "Definitely light in the loafers."

"All I know is he never came on to me. Even when we were alone in a hotel and drinking Mai Tais." That was from JBarcoLo who, remembering that conversation, slipped one hand behind her to cop an exploratory feel of her left buttock as she nodded in a way that suggested the group should take my not coming on to her as a definite test of sexual preference.

Tall Tina added, "He doesn't seem to keep any female staff members."

If only she knew that my mistake was simply hiring women of child-bearing age.

That's when Basso Pesci chimed in. "I worked for the company for eleven years, and it used to be that we'd have events for our big customers where we'd put on these, whatyoucallums, these... plays... these *skits*, that's the word. I was in charge for three of them. And every time Cheeseley volunteered to play a woman. And I mean vol-un-teered. It can be funny to have a guy wearing a dress and having giant... you know... melons. But with a normal guy you have to persuade them, ease them into the idea. Not Cheeseley. His hand was up right from the start. Couldn't wait to slip on that big brassiere."

Well. It's true, I volunteered. Why? Because I knew I would get big laughs. It's comic gold. Ask Tom Hanks or Dustin Hoffman or a hundred other manly men who've worked the cross-dressing gag.

The others added varying levels of agreement, and I watched as Reggie sneaked another glance at the mirror and winked. Then I got it. By asking about the possibility of my being gay he'd switched off the anger in the room. He'd de-demonized me, and that was as close to being humanized as I could have hoped at that moment.

Tell Me If I'm Being Paranoid

So, OUR FOCUS GROUP—our failed sting operation—was over. What could I conclude? I found myself believing that while any one of them could, with encouragement, work up some contempt toward me, I could *not* believe *anyone* in that room would actually assault me. Sure, they'd talked about slashing tires, but mostly they'd bandied about insults—pederast Catholic priests, for Christ's sake—yet I walked out feeling light, and yes I was wearing loafers, but I walked out sanguine, feeling safe. At some level these people understood that I was no villain. While they might hold a grudge, they wouldn't hold a gun. And yet this happened...

...you tell me if I'm being paranoid...

I live in a condo complex in Chandler, an easy drive from the focus group facility in Tempe. When I got home there was a car blocking the driveway to my unit. It wasn't in my driveway, but parked in front of it, so that when I tried to turn in, I realized that I wasn't going to fit past. The problem was a big American car, a Chrysler I think it was, one of the boxy ones with narrow side windows. In this case, the narrow windows were effectively blacked out with window tint. I couldn't tell if someone was inside so I rolled down my window and listened and yes, the engine was running. I gave a tap on my horn, as if they might have somehow missed my headlights with my car angled toward them a couple of feet from their rear fender. But the car didn't move. Then a second car pulled behind me and I felt trapped—and I literally was, unable to go forward or backward. Despite having just declared myself safe from employee violence, I felt the fear rise up when both doors of the car in front opened and out came two young men, lean men with tight t-shirts over athletic muscles, one carrying a black object heavy enough to affect his weight distribution, maybe a whopping wrench. They wore baseball caps on heads angled down so that their faces were in shadows.

I double-checked the locks on my doors then pulled out my cellphone and, as I dialed 911, glanced to make sure I could see the license plate. There wasn't one.

That's when yet another car came toward us from the opposite direction. Both hatted heads spun around and their bodies followed. They jumped back in the car and drove off, while the car behind me reversed and vanished. The approaching car turned out to be driven by a neighbor, Mrs. Misanni, who rolled down her window and waited for me to do likewise before yelling imperiously, "No parking on the street. Don't make me report you again."

I yelled back, "I want to kiss you, Mrs. Misanni."

"Prick."

At least I think that's what she replied; I wasn't waiting to be certain. I zipped up my window and lurched into my garage and waited for the door to close before I unlocked my car doors. A carjacking? It seemed to me the essence of a good carjacking was to sneak up on the driver's door from the blind spot and jerk it open before the person had time to lock the doors or lift a cell phone. Didn't these guys get any training at all?

Or maybe it was just a robbery. There was one thing of which I could be certain—those could not have been angry ex-employees of Mundane Industries. We had not laid off anyone that young and well built except Rafa, and

I would have recognized him. So I persuaded myself that the incident was not related to the office.

I decided that it if they could be chased away by little Mrs. Misanni, they couldn't be serious criminals. I would wash the incident out of my mind. After all, I had enough worries in there already. It was time to have a talk with Putin and get some confidence back.

One Headless Messenger
In All of History

THE NEXT MORNING Reggie was waiting in my office, ready to discuss what he would do next.

"Nothing," I insisted brightly.

"Ah, Win, don't be pissy. I only pushed them to see if I could get one to tip-off something about a cartridge."

"It's not that. You were great. You were so great that I am convinced that they don't really blame me. I feel liberated." I bounced around in my desk chair, a free bird.

He looked unconvinced. "I'm glad you're feeling frisky. But I don't know. That cartridge was an act of aggression. I agree it probably wasn't anyone in that group, but last night you got to see how the inner rage is there and it's real. I still have dozens of other suspects."

"I know. And you're right about the anger. But it isn't that kind of anger. Yes, they compared us in HR to IRS agents and car salesmen and even priests, but nobody's out killing car salesmen or priests, much less me. They're disgusted, but they aren't going to ruin their lives for a bit of revenge from someone who was only indirectly involved. I was the messenger. You hear that thing about shooting the messenger, but nobody ever really shoots the messenger, right?"

Reggie, a history buff, then informed me that in the first century BC, when Tigranes of Armenia, the King of Kings, was told that a Roman army was approaching, he had the head of the messenger cut off, which naturally meant that from then on he got only good news, which eventually cost him his kingdom.

This seemed to me to reinforce my point, even though Reggie tried to sound stern as he concluded, "There's a lesson there for you, Win."

"Yeah. That there's one headless messenger in all of history. I like my odds."

He said "No" in a way that made it clear that what he meant was "No, you idiot." He added, "I'm referring to overconfidence. About only getting the good news. Do that, and you lose. It's the bad news that can kill you."

"I just can't work up any fear anymore. And can I tell you something that sounds crazy? I miss it. When I was worried about being shot, all my other worries seemed inconsequential. Now I'm back to all my old worries."

"You want me to scare you?"

I laughed. "No, but thanks. You've been terrific. A real friend."

"Unless you give me a direct order to the contrary, I'm going to keep my investigation going. Quietly. In my spare time."

"Don't ever let Mr. Cone hear you say *spare time*."

What were all my old worries that were flooding back? There was...

... the danger of having my department outsourced and my job then eliminated.

... Genghis Cone treating me as an escort service for his daughter and her ambitions.

... Carlota believing I lusted after her, and who could blame her? In Genghis' office sat an alarming photo of the two of us that did nothing to contradict the notion that I found her throbbingly desirable.

... Eve, who I quite possibly loved and who didn't know it and who I seemed incapable of connecting with while Genghis employed her.

... my lack of a staff, with just two employees, FullOf-Himself and Eileen, doing the work of four that should have been at least six—better yet, eight.

No wonder I missed the distraction of contemplating who'd want to shoot me.

The Toilet In the Ladies'
Is Overflowing

M Y FIRST BOSS ONCE SAID TO ME, "What's the most important step in climbing a mountain?"

"The first one," I answered confidently, expecting a lecture on getting started.

"No. The last one. If you can figure out how to get to the last one, you'll have figured them all out."

That struck me as profound, and I've recalled it many times over the years. Trying to apply it to my current situation left me perplexed. What would be my last step? I did a visualization exercise and saw myself accepting the HR Person of the Year Award while my new wife Eve sat grinning with pride, laughing at my casual brilliance as I gave my acceptance speech.

That beautiful thought was interrupted by one of the clerks from Accounting walking into my office and saying, "The toilet in the Ladies' is overflowing."

Concealing my annoyance, I asked sweetly, "And why would you be telling me about it? That would be Facilities."

"Yeah, I know. But they don't answer, and my boss said you'd know what to do."

REASON #24: Restrooms.

That reminds me...

We have a lovely young man who's a manager in our

shipping department. That sounds like someone who makes sure the people packing up cardboard boxes are doing it right. In this case, it's much more technological and financial, working through the logistics of getting our products in the right places as efficiently as possible. He was Allen when he was hired... he's now becoming Amber.

Perhaps you've encountered someone who's undergone the transgender transition. Fascinating. You see what the hormone injections do and you think differently about the nature of sexuality. Just don't think about the surgery part, which I just did and I'm crossing my legs and squeezing them together and still feeling creeped out and mildly nauseous. Maybe that's why a number of men have decided they don't like hanging out with Allen/ Amber. You see a guy on TV get whacked in the nuts and you can't help but hunch over and moan; that's how some men react just seeing him walk by, which does nothing good for productivity.

But that's not why I had to get involved. I wish I could just say lightly, "To each his... or her... own," and refuse to get involved. But no, not in HR. There are laws and threats of lawsuits, and one call to the police...

Up until last year, you'd look at Allen and think... well, you probably wouldn't look at Allen, or if you did, it wouldn't provoke any particular thoughts. Ordinary. If you forced yourself to study him, you might note that if he were to lie on his back, he'd be rather flat, like an Angelfish on its side. His skin is smooth, seemingly poreless, and his hair is curly, too tightly curled for his liking, and he uses chemicals on it. But even noting those details make his appearance seem out of the ordinary, which it wasn't. If you got to know him you'd like him because he's bashful and sweet-natured and perhaps a touch feminine, but nothing that would make you think there's a woman in there yearning to get out. He was more dainty than feminine, although he's always gotten manicures, which I know is fashionable in some circles but always seemed to me to be the first step in cross-dressing.

Allen came to me a year ago and asked for an appointment with me. At the time we had four of us in the department, and I wasn't handling routine employee issues so I deflected him. But he pleaded to meet with me, me alone. Because he once worked a few offices down from mine, I'd gotten to know him a bit, so I was curious.

It was charming-sad to see him struggle to confess his secret, starting with a hesitant, "This is really, really hard to talk about."

Having been through many confessions, I could have helped, making it a game of 20 Questions, starting with guesses so outrageous that the truth seemed mild. ("Is there a dead body in the trunk of your car?") However, I've learned to hold back and listen. Why? To see him struggle.

That sounds cruel, but no, my motives run the opposite direction. I believe it's important for people to learn to confess whatever it is about themselves that they've been afraid to say. I wanted to let Allen practice somewhere safe, with me.

He got it out and he cried and I reassured and I promised. Little did I know what I was in for, but still there are times when we in HR get the chance to be so deeply human and this was one of them.

What I knew but hadn't given much attention was that dealing with transgender employees was an issue working itself out all over the country.

(I'm going to digress here. Consider it a test: If you really are meant for a career in HR, this should be riveting history.)

One of the first big transgender cases was called Jane Doe v. Boeing. The HR folks at Boeing had tried to cooperate with their Jane Doe and with, get this, the *eight other employees* in some stage of "sex reassignment." So they came up with a policy, unwritten at first, but then, as is inevitable, it became written. Why inevitable? Because as soon as you enforce the policy, someone will get "written up," and that means you have to specify the offense.

REASON #25: Write one policy; make a hundred enemies.

This is going back a couple of decades, but as I recall Boeing's policies dealt with the tricky part of sex-reassignment. You don't just leave on vacation as John Doe, get an implant and a dress and come back as Jane Doe. Instead, you are to spend a year living as a member of the opposite sex. So you have John dressing as Jane and that's how we get into the restroom dilemma. Picture John-now-Jane wobbling on new high heels into the Women's room. How would female users feel about that? They might be flattered, perhaps welcoming Jane as a new member of the team. Nope. They complained. To HR, of course.

They might have been sympathetic to Jane, but when it came to the Women's room, they were unyielding: No Peckers Allowed.

So what to do? In the Boeing case, Jane Doe agreed to use the restroom at a nearby fast food restaurant, and the HR folks instituted a policy decreeing that during the year-long transition that Jane dress in gender-neutral clothing in order not to distract/confuse/annoy fellow employees.

Jane Doe could not help him/herself, however. Jane showed up wearing a string of pink pearls, and that was it—axed. She sued and lost, then won on appeal, only to lose again at the state supreme court.

This is what happens to us in HR; it isn't that we make rules with which it is difficult to comply, but there are employees who need a rule to enable them to know just how to *not* comply and blame you for making the rule. Where will it all end? Perhaps with a row of Porta-Johns in the parking lot.

> **REASON #26:** When you write a policy, you have shown those of rebellious spirit just how little they have to do to stick you with the unseemly duty of enforcing your policy, and thus they know just how to make you look silly.

By the way, since the time of Jane Doe v. Boeing, there have been a string of other cases and with them an interesting development known as the "Principle of Least Astonishment." Don't you love that name? The idea is that an employee should use the restroom that most fits his/her "presentation." I find that astonishingly logical. However, a federal appeals court said that if another employee complained, then the employer would have to accommodate the complainer by making available some other restroom. Fine. But hold on… that restroom can't be too far away or you'll violate OSHA rules that every employee has access to a convenient restroom, and while we don't know exactly what "convenient" means, we know that a quarter of a mile was held not to qualify. Sigh.

Meanwhile, back to my tender young employee, Allen/Amber. She had begun her year of living as a female and was now just Amber to me, and "she" or "her." I felt a special closeness to her after her double confession: first, her confiding in me about her plans for sex reassignment; then later telling me that I was the first person she'd told. That sort of thing creates a bond. Perhaps I let that bond cloud my vision about her situation, because I had jumped in to defend her against those who were troubled by her... what to call it... her *eccentric* appearance. I'm sorry to have to tell you that she was not the comeliest of cross-dressers, with something asymmetrical about her face and body. I couldn't shake the impression that a Picasso painting of an Angelfish had come to life.

"I'm so sorry to bring you another problem, Win," Amber said sweetly, fiddling with her chunky red necklace.

"That's why I'm here."

"I was in the Women's room, and that awful Big Connie from Customer Service who has been a pain in my butt starting with my first lipstick came in and insisted that I had to leave. But I'd just gotten there, and I was desperate to go, and I mean desperate. So I told her I wouldn't be but a minute and I slipped into one of the stalls. She was bitchy about it and insisted I leave, but I went ahead and did my business, which takes a while longer in these clothes. While I'm sitting in there, I hear her call the police. She told them she wanted to report a pervert in the ladies' room. A pervert? I'm the one sitting in there minding my own business behind a closed door. A pervert? Like I was in there waiting and hoping she'd walk her pimply ass in there and drop her slacks. So I told her that if I wanted to see something like her ass that I'd buy myself one of those waffle-foam mattress toppers and glue it to the back of a Volkswagen and..."

"Amber. Hold on. Did she actually call the police or was she just pretending, just talking into her cellphone without dialing?"

"She called. I could hear the dispatcher asking her questions, but it just sounded like a chipmunk or something from where I was, but they must have told her to leave the restroom because she did."

"Did the police show up to talk to you?"

"Not yet."

"OK. If they show up, I'll tell the front desk to refer them to me. And I'll explain what's going on. They may want you to make a statement. If so, do *not* go into a tirade. Just say that you're following your doctor's orders to live as a woman and that you have a legal right to use the restroom. That'll confuse them. Meanwhile, I'll talk to Connie again and see if I can't find a way to resolve things. I'll talk to her first, then the three of us can meet."

"My hero," she said in falsetto, overdoing the feminine. I wanted to tell her that not all women can play the ingénue but I let it be.

I gave instructions to the front desk before calling to instruct Big Connie to come right to my office. (Connie isn't huge or anything; she got stuck with Big Connie to distinguish her from Little Connie, who used to work in the same department and was practically a dwarf.)

I let Connie vent, then tried to slowly turn her thinking around, explaining the agonies of being trapped inside the wrong gender and the year of living-as and all the rest.

"Well, that's real liberal of you, real open-minded."

I started to thank her for the compliment but spotted the smirk and realized she was being sarcastic. "So," she continued, "why don't I tell that freak to just come up here and use the washroom by your office? How would that be?"

That would be just fine. Not bad. "I wish I'd thought of it. We'll make the restroom in HR the official accommodations for those with... how shall I put it?..."

REASON #27: Always having to choose words so carefully that you spend half your day groping around for neutral terms. Positively neutral. That's us.

"… unique requirements." I beamed. This was a good idea. We in HR would lead the way.

She scoffed. "So it won't be a Men's, and it won't be a Ladies'. So what'll you put on the door? 'Other'? 'Miscellaneous'? 'Not Sure'?"

Well, she had me there, but in the end she agreed to tell the police that the issue had been resolved. Another victory for the win-win spirit.

Sometimes You Have
to Shoot a Hostage

MOMENTS AFTER THAT VICTORY, as I was studying a report on excess use of exclamation points in company communications, I got a call from lovely Eve, telling me I was needed in Mr. Cone's office. "Please hurry," she whispered.

When I arrived, there were two uniformed Phoenix PD officers sitting with Mr. Cone, both looking like they'd played high school football, not too many years ago. I wouldn't want to try to block either one.

They had arrived to investigate the great Ladies' Room Pervert Caper, and when the front desk couldn't reach the supposed victim, Connie—she'd been with me, but no one knew that—they'd asked to speak to the head of the company, who turned to me, of course.

REASON #28: The Defaulted: It's the place you call when you don't know where to call.

This gave me, the Great Explainer, the chance to do my best while we waited for Eve to get Big Connie. I earnestly explained the new plan, to make the restroom near HR available and to be the new example for openness. The cops didn't seem too impressed, but perhaps they've been schooled to contain their emotions.

When Connie arrived they told Genghis and me that they wanted to speak to her alone, and so they went into

Mr. Cone's private conference room.

As soon as they were gone, he turned on me with some pointed comments about my failure to contain the situation. He actually growled at me.

"The first thing I did," I said in my defense, "was to give instructions to the front desk to send the police to me. I don't know why that didn't happen."

"Find out and fire whoever screwed up."

"I don't want to overreact, certainly not till I know the circumstances, but I assure you..."

"I don't want your assurances. And I don't give a shit who's on the front desk. I want you to show some balls. I want you to make heads roll. You can't be a vice-president of this company and have people get away with ignoring your instructions."

"I agree, but there may be a reasonable explanation."

"Maybe there is, but that doesn't mean you have to be reasonable. Sometimes you have to shoot a hostage."

What a horrid thought. Horrid. That should have been my cue to just shut up and hope that he forgot about the whole thing. (Half of corporate life is politics and half of politics is delay.) Instead, I foolishly debated the point, ignoring all the signs that Mr. Cone had gone full-Genghis and had passed beyond any hope of reasoning with him. "Yes, but you hired me to prevent disputes, to be the one who understands and keep things from getting out of control. That's my job."

"Your job is to deal with all the petty bullshit so it *doesn't distract the people who really matter.*"

That stung. I'd spent years getting used to the cracks and slights but never something like this.

Genghis could see that he had gone too far. He's not insensitive; he just pretends to be. The asshole.

"Shit," he said, the anger imploded. "That came out

wrong." He looked confused. "Carlota tells me that I need to learn how to apologize, but I don't have much experience."

I shrugged, the very mention of Carlota confusing the issue.

He waved his mechanical pencil in the air and said, "Tell me what I should say."

"You want me to apologize to me?"

"Yeah. What would be a great apology?"

"I'm not sure what to tell you." We stared at each other, and I blinked, my need to accommodate and educate over-riding my hurt feelings. "In the movie *As Good As It Gets*, Jack Nicholson has fallen for Helen Hunt and he takes her out to dinner and stupidly insults the dress she's wearing. She stands up and says, 'Give me a compliment quick, Melvin, or I'm leaving.' And he says, 'You make me want to be a better man' which may be the finest compliment ever offered anyone. And she melts back into her seat and says, 'That's the nicest thing anybody ever said to me.' He says, "Maybe I overshot a bit. I just wanted you to sit down.'"

"I remember that movie. It had a dog. So I'm supposed to say that you make me want to be a better man?"

"No. But you come up with a compliment that's more good than the insult was bad. You tell me that I'm the best thing to happen to the company and you hope I'll always be with you. Then, if you really want to practice being large, you put that in a note and enclose a five hundred dollar Visa gift card."

"I know you're joking. But..." He opened his desk and pawed around in a drawer. "Here." He passed me an enve-lope that said in gold script, "A gift for you." When I looked up, he explained, "It's along those lines but more me."

I was touched. At that instant I felt that we were indeed developing a mutual respect. I put the envelope in my pocket and he gave me a manly nod, and I gave him one back, and we were okay.

"Well then, moving on, I was going to call you up here anyway. We need to talk about Carlota."

That's when the police returned and informed us that Big Connie had backed my version of events and that they considered the matter satisfactorily concluded. Genghis walked them to his door, giving me a chance to glance inside the envelope he just given me. It was a gift card for $10 at Dunkin' Donuts... but that $10 applied only if I spent at least $20. "More me," he'd said. Yes, it was.

He resumed his place behind his big desk and said, "About Carlota. She tells me that she enjoyed her evening with you."

"Same here." I put on my well-worn expression of delight. I hadn't seen Carlota since our evening together and I'd put her out of my mind.

"I told her not to get too attached, but that was probably a mistake because she usually does the opposite of whatever I tell her to do. Still, what can you do?"

"If the parents had let Romeo and Juliet date for a while, she would have gotten sick of him moping around."

He ignored that gem, probably didn't even hear it.

"Here's my point: I'm going to let you be her escort again. This time it's meeting with investors from Dubai who insist on meeting in Vegas. I can't go, so Carlota is representing us. I don't like her being alone with these guys, so you're there to make sure nothing goes wrong."

"More of a bodyguard."

He made a noise like when you pull your foot out of mud. "The less time you spend thinking about her body, the better. The deal is that one of these guys has a son he wanted to set up with Carlota. I think he thought it was like the old Mafia days when you intermarried to try to keep from having families go to war. When I told her about it she insisted on me informing them that she's about to get engaged. So you'll be there to play the role of lovebird. I wouldn't have thought you'd be able to pull that off, but..." He turned and pulled the picture of me dancing with Carlota from under a file folder on his credenza. "I still don't believe this." He stared at the photo with an intensity that was a tad creepy.

Meanwhile, I distracted myself by picturing myself as an actual lovebird, flying about Carlota. That image transformed into a Cessna circling a battleship. There I was, a Cessna in a storm, not wanting to land but what was the option?

Then she entered, Eve the Perfect. She was wearing a fitted suit of amber satin that stopped above her knee, which I shouldn't have been looking at, so I gave myself an excuse by complimenting her shoes, which was slightly absurd because they were the simplest of beige mules... if mules is the term I want. Open in the back. Why "mule," one of nature's dullest, sturdiest creatures?

She gave me the lowest wattage on the rheostat of her smile and hurried to inform Mr. Cone that Senator Lockman was on the phone. That was the Senator I'd met just a few nights ago, the husband of my Mad Joan.

I stood to exit, but he waved me back into my seat. "No biggie. He'll just hit me up for a contribution to something, probably his reelection."

As I watched Eve leave, my thoughts drifted to this odd confluence of my sexual being. Here I sat...

Win-Win Cheeseley, a man nearly everyone assumed was gay,

while on the desk in front of me sat a photo of me dancing with a woman and sporting a... well, sporting a lump that wasn't in my throat,

while the woman of my dream life was gliding out of

the office with my eyes chasing after her,

while my boss was on the phone with the senator-husband of a woman I'd slept with just days before.

Gay, my ass.

These pleasant thoughts were interrupted by the realization that Genghis had just swiveled toward me while saying, "It happens that he's right here with me, discussing a case that is highly relevant... Yes, I'll tell him... I'm sure he'll make us proud... Yes, I'm sure he'd be delighted to contribute to the campaign... And congratulations on the renewal of wedding vows. I saw pictures in the paper... You always make me laugh, Senator."

I noted that he hadn't laughed.

He put down the receiver and shook his head. "I don't like my employees getting wrapped up in volunteer work, and here the Senator is talking about you as running his LPGA committee or whatever it is—the Mixed Nuts group."

"It's LBGT, and he cornered me. What could I say?"

"You're always telling me you aren't gay. What about saying that?"

I couldn't explain that Mad Joan had used my supposed gayness as a cover story for us being seen together. "I wish I had." True.

He looked down when he sighed and saw the picture of me with his daughter. "You aren't bisexual, are you? That's the worst."

"No. I'm not L or G or B or T. Just plain old H."

He goggled at me. "H for hetero," I explained.

"Well, stay in the closet a while longer. I'm trying to let the investment community see you and Carlota as romantically involved and so I want you to find a way to get out of being on that committee."

"Great. I'll think of something."

One Foot On Either
Side of the Bar

E AGER TO CHANGE THE SUBJECT, I turned to the boss's
favorite one: "I just saw the latest financials. Congratulations. It was a great quarter, especially household
products."

"Yeah, we need to talk about financials. They were
good, but not good enough. We're going to have to tighten
things up."

What tightened was my stomach. Whenever Genghis
Cone talked about tightening, he meant budget cuts, and
that meant more lay-offs. I tried to make a joke of it.
"We've had a hiring freeze for so long that our teams are
getting freezer burn."

"Whose side on you on, Cheeseley?"

Isn't that the Big Question for those of us in HR? We
try to be on both sides, to help the company by helping
employees, but the result is that we have one foot on
either side of the bar... the bar upper management keeps
raising. "You know me, Chief, on the side of maximum
productivity. We're running like a finely-tuned engine.
We want to keep it oiled."

"I count on you for oil. And I want you to get us a better
deal on it. I need you to come up with a plan to reduce
employee costs by ten percent next year. And, here is
where it gets good. I want you to reduce costs ten percent while we have a ten percent increase in sales. There's

the sort of challenge that gives me a hard-on." Without intending to do so, both of us glanced at the photo.

This is the sort of pronouncement that executives love to make. They toss out an assignment like turning over a Magic 8 Ball. I want this. Make it happen. If you can't, I'll get someone who will.

I knew not to challenge him on one of his challenges. If I did, he would cite one of his standard examples, probably the one about President Kennedy decreeing that the U.S. would land a man on the moon—I know, it should have been "person," or better yet, "American"—by the end of the decade. That was indeed a great challenge, and it enlivened the nation's spirit. But JFK had the Red Scare to give him leeway, and he backed the challenge with big budgets for NASA. But no point in arguing, so I gave him what I wanted to hear. "That is going to be a huge challenge."

"Are you up to it?"

I wasn't. Perhaps I'd simply charged up too many hills to think this one would hold some fresh view. But you don't become one of the leading HR professionals in the state without learning how to keep doubts to yourself. "It a big goal, yes, but I'm the ma... person for the job."

Eve was in the outer office as I left and I forced myself to apologize to her. "I'm sorry about saying something about your shoes."

She frowned. Adorable. "You decided you don't like them? I think they're the wrong brown."

"No, they're great. It's just that we have a policy against complimenting personal appearance. It causes a lot of problems."

She took a minute, deciding if I was putting her on. I forget how stupid some of our HR policies sound.

REASON #29: Having a policy on compliments.

"That's right. I remember that one from our onboarding class. But, Win, you can break that policy with me any time you like."

That's when Putin—where had he been?—sauntered into the room behind her, smoking a dark cigarette. He bent over to check out her shoes, or more likely her legs, because he did one of those O-face pull-backs.

"In that case..." I began.

I was going to tell her how perfect her legs were and then work my way up from there, but twenty plus years of HR training stopped me. I just couldn't overcome a life of caution.

Putin gestured for me to continue, but I couldn't. "If only..." I started and stopped.

"I understand," she said. "You are involved with Carlota and you shouldn't be noticing other women."

Genghis yelled for her, and she stood. With a teasing look, she said, "And I'm sure you won't notice this suit, but it's new. I treated myself because of my new raise and promotion."

Raise? Promotion? Any raises or promotions had to be approved by me. Before I could ask, she was gone, leaving me with a disgusted Putin. "For your sake, I'm going to fuck her myself."

"Don't say that."

"Yes, for your sake. Not to my taste. I like them big and sturdy so I can wade in like the surf. Did I say that right? No matter. I do this for you. So you can have, what you business guys call a case study, no? You see how I handle it and you learn."

"No. And it would never happen. You're not her type, either."

"Her type is the rich type. Go over there and eavesdrop on her flirting with the big boss."

"She's friendly with everybody."

"Not everybody gives her raises. She bought that new dress to celebrate the promotion and new salary."

"That can't be right. I see every change in payroll.

"You were off in San Diego. So the boss calls in your junior, the one who thinks he's a cowboy and an Indian, that FullOfShit."

"FullOfHimself. And that's impossible."

"You ask. You learn. Then, you take my case study."

The Demon Inside Me

ON THE WAY BACK TO MY OFFICE I spotted FullOf-Himself in T-position, that is, hunched over, texting. There's a whole generation who will one day make chiropractors rich.

"My office. Now."

He took his time, but came in still looking at his phone and asking "Whatsup, Doc?"

I got right to telling him I'd heard the rumor about Eve's raise going through without my signature.

He finally looked up. He admitted it. Proudly. "All true. The big man had me come right up to the big office, and I took care of him, jingo bingo, wingo wango."

I explained how he had done a disservice to me, the department and even to poor Eve. Instead of withering in the chair, cowering and begging forgiveness, he shrugged.

"I think you're overanalyzing. In fact, Mr. Cone thinks you do that a lot. The word he used was anal, which I thought was a bit harsh. I don't think it affects your work."

"I have no idea what that means. And I can't believe that you'd criticize me to our CEO. That's a firing offense."

"I just sat there. He was the one criticizing. Besides, I don't think he'd let you fire me. He said I was the future of the company."

"That's absurd."

"No, we were kicking around ideas, and he was impressed."

"What ideas were you kicking around?"

"I told him how I'm working on a project to have more remote employees. How it would save a lot of money. You know."

It was all I could do not to reach over and slap his self-satisfied face. That was *my* plan, my big back-up plan. "Yes, I know. I'm the one who gave you all the data to assemble." It was part of a major initiative I'd been saving for the next round of cost-cutting, the very one that had come up today.

"Well, he liked it. And he likes me. I read a post the other day about how important it is to personal branding to have a nickname. I kinda like the The Future. Cool. Go ahead. Try it out. Just say it and see how it fits."

"Your immediate future is going to be sneaking your resume onto the company copy machines if you ever go behind my back again."

"Your back? You were off in San Diego, and the boss called me and wanted my help."

I think of FullOfHimself as dim, but then occasionally I realize that he isn't dumb; he just limits his mental energy to what interests him, which is, of course, him. His next sentence startled me with its political savvy: "Next time you're not around and he wants something, I'll tell him that you said I couldn't talk to him and that he had to call you. Is that what you want?"

Suddenly I wasn't sure what I wanted, other than to lie down for a nap.

Then, sensing my vacillation, FullOfHimself moved in. "I know this seems soon to someone old, but sudden is the new cautious. I want to apply for the job of Assistant Director. A new title will give me more credibility."

"That's ridiculous. You haven't even been here a year."

"That's what I told Mr. Cone, but he liked the idea."

"So it's like that, is it?"

"Like what?"

To be honest, I wasn't sure. I'd heard that expression somewhere, in movies perhaps, but put on the spot, I couldn't be certain what it meant. "The point is…" I wasn't sure what the point was. But I didn't learn the art of corporate politicking for nothing. "I'll go to bat for you. I'll sit down with Mr. Cone and see if I can't get you a new title."

He held out his fist and I gave it a bump, but it was a lie. What was this demon that had taken up residence inside me?

There Will Be Consequences

THE ODDEST THING...

Last night as I was driving home from the office, I saw a dark car exactly like the one blocking my driveway the other night, and it was following me. I went around the block to see if it was overactive imagination, but nope, there it was, still tailing me.

I called Reggie on my cellphone to ask for advice. He's amazing. No hesitation. He said that he was at a store near my condo and instructed me to head straight home and he'd be waiting, armed, when I arrived.

"If they rear-end you at a streetlight, just drive on. Do not get out of the car, no matter what. Just keep going. If they try to pull alongside you, they may fire at you. So hit the brakes and then accelerate. Stay low. Are you nervous?"

"I admit it, I am a little."

"Good. The adrenaline is your friend if you use it right. Are they right behind you or are they hanging back?"

"They are behind the car that's behind me."

"Good. If they stay that way, then they probably won't take you out while you're driving. Keep in bunches of cars. Now hang up the phone and concentrate, but call if anything changes."

I told myself that this might just be a good thing. In detective novels, the tough guy PI always finds a way to confront the bad guys. Usually the case is at a complete dead-end, and whap, right when he's about to give up, some villain appears and threatens him, thereby offering up a new set of clues to follow and probably a good punch-up. This sudden turn of events never seems terribly believable, but then the realistic situation, running through all the clues and the case petering out, would not make for a satisfying detective novel, much less a series with motion picture potential.

Mine turned out to be the realistic situation; that is, a petering out. Just as I made the final turn into my condo complex, the dark car sped up and kept going straight. Strange. I wasn't sure if I should be relieved or disappointed not to have a confrontation with Reggie backing me up. Wait a minute... Reggie.

He and his gun were hiding in the shadows, and that was now my replacement fear—after all, in his seventies, his vision could not be the sharpest. As I pulled into the driveway, I hit the garage door opener and turned on the dome lights in my car so he could see it was me. Then I pulled in and got out slowly, hands raised, just in case.

That's when there was a shout at the corner of the garage, and I jumped. But it was just Mrs. Misanni, the Neighborhood Watch Captain, going into a rant, "Your friend parked on the street. These are private streets with no parking. Did you not get the warnings?" Before I could respond, she piled on threats. "I'm going to have to report you to the Board this time. There will be *consequences*!" She said the last bit with a sandpapery intensity and must have liked the sound of that last word because she banged it along a second time.

"Sorry, Mrs. M. It was a bit of an emergency."

"Ha!"

She pointed at my chest... no, not my chest. She pointed twice, once on each side. I saw that my hands were still up and my armpits soaked from the anxiety of the drive home.

"A laundry emergency?"

She threw in a snort, and as she turned to leave, ran straight into Reggie stealthily angling around the corner of the garage.

As they untangled, she noticed the pistol he was holding at his side and grew interested. Turns out that her late husband had an extensive gun collection. The two of them dropped into gun talk, and that led to her invitation to have a look at the dead guy's collection. Reggie said he'd be at her place in ten minutes. "Just as soon as I tuck Winslow here into bed and move my car."

"You can park in my driveway anytime." Perhaps it was the hype of adrenaline, but I'd swear she was doing a Mae West voice.

I Have a Surprise for You

I WAS RUNNING LATE but, even so, the Chihuly glass in the ceiling of the lobby of the Bellagio in Las Vegas stopped me cold. I stood and marveled. I saw an interview with Chihuly where he referred to the glass pieces as "flowers" and the curving rods of the metal structure holding them as "stems," which surprised me, because I had seen it before and decided it was an underwater scene.

There are hundreds of pieces of glass, perhaps over a thousand. I couldn't imagine what it must have cost. But I could imagine what rooms at the hotel cost. I'd once arranged a suite here so Mr. Cone could host a cocktail party for attendees of a retailers' conference. The suite, not even a thousand square feet, cost $1600 for the one night, and that was before taxes, not to mention the cocktails. I had sneaked in peanuts and pretzels from Costco, and that probably saved a hundred bucks.

What also saved a few hundred bucks was that while Genghis stayed in the suite, his assistant—this was long before Eve—had booked me into a place called Goldstrike or Goldspike... Goldsomething. While the Bellagio was $1600, my room was $23. A friendly kid I met in the elevator told me that his room smelled of sour milk, "But," he concluded cheerily, "for nine bucks a night, I can take the stank." Nine bucks! I got screwed at 23 bucks? Nine? You can't rent a chain saw for a day for nine dollars, a tool I wished I thought to rent for that night so as to be able to slice off the sticky top layer of the nightstand.

But I'm getting off the subject, which was my trip to Las Vegas to act as faux boyfriend of the aggressively undesirable Carlota Cone. I was startled when I got my travel plans from our travel person. (The company doesn't allow you to make your own arrangements, for fear you might overlook, say, a $23 a night hotel. Little did they know they'd been out-shopped by a teenager from Wisconsin. They also don't want you to overlook the flight to Chicago that makes three stops and arrives at 2AM but saves the company $12 in airfare. You won't be surprised to learn the travel department is known internally as HAB, for Hell And Back. I once made the mistake of suggesting to Genghis that we might give a bit more thought to the productivity loss that comes with lowest-cost travel, especially the brutal flight schedules. I could tell he was unmoved, so I confided the nickname Hell And Back. He laughed and said, "Perfect. Don't change a thing. We want employees to dread travel for the company—think of how much money that saves every year.")

Still, there I was at the Bellagio, and after admiring the Chihuly and giving my name at the registration desk, the young woman from, I'd guess, South America, straightened her posture. "Oh, you don't want to check in here. You're in one of the Penthouse Suites. There's a separate check in area for you at the Executive Suite Lounge." She checked her watch, a giant one with a white rubber strap. "You just made it. It closes in twenty minutes, at nine."

There was such awe in her voice speaking of the lounge that I felt I should give her the chance to express herself on the subject. "Nice, is it?"

"Just the carpet alone. You'll want to lie down and roll around. And notice the walls. They're leather. Handstitched. And there's food and drinks. If I ever get married

I want to stay in one of the suites."

I offered her my prediction that she'd have a line of candidates for her hand, then went to find this travelers' Valhalla. And, yes, the check-in area was lovely, and the walls were leather, but why would someone brag that they were hand-stitched? The thought of some poor sluggo stitching the pieces together nagged at me, and I almost missed the free chocolate covered strawberries.

> **REASON #30: Spend enough time with workers and you start to wonder if any luxury is worth the human cost it takes to make the thing.**

> **REASON #31: Thinking in terms of "labor" and "human cost" when you ought to be admiring the grand outcome and thinking, "Oh, yes, this is where I belong."**

Speaking of not belonging, I soon learned that the suite wasn't mine, but Carlota's and that I was staying with her. Hearing that from the desk clerk was almost enough to make me drop the spare chocolate-covered strawberry I was balancing on a black cloth napkin while signing in.

Trying, as always, to sound chipper, I asked the slender young man in giant spectacles, "How many beds in that room?"

"It's two bedrooms and two baths. Nearly 2000 square feet. I hope you'll find it adequate, but I can check on the availability of the larger ones, if required."

I gave him a look that told him I knew he was being a smartass about it and that I didn't hold it against him.

Although he gave me a keycard for the room, when I got there I felt obligated to ring the doorbell and wait.

Perhaps it was the stress of recent events, but I swear that when the door opened my first impression was that the hotel was so swank that the room came with trained polar bears as butlers. In reality, it was Carlota in a giant white robe and towel around her head.

She seemed pleased to see me, which I couldn't remember ever being true at the offices of Mundane Industries. "Good timing. I just got out of the shower." She smelled the back of her hand then offered it to me. "Great soap. Check it out."

It was a fragrance that was like the room—it screamed that it would never ever scream, that it would merely whisper, "Admire me, mortal." There were floor-to-ceiling windows out to the carnival barker lights of Vegas. The floors were marble, and there were two rugs, one to define the living room space and the other for the dining room, with a table for six. The woods were dark walnut, the carpets and curtains camel and cranberry, with colorful artwork on every wall, including a single Chihuly flower mounted between the windows.

Carlota was not herself, which is to say she was chatty and girlish. After she'd told me of her trip and her plans for the meetings in the morning, she said, with mischief in her voice and eyes, "I have a surprise for you."

That's when she stood and started toward a closed door, most certainly one of the bedrooms. I hesitated. I realized I hadn't prepared for the no-sex conversation. She gave me an impatient wave, and I reluctantly followed, my mind frantically reviewing avoidance gambits.

She opened the door slowly, and in soft light I could see a bed, and then, someone sleeping in it. Creeping up on some unsuspecting sleeper violated my sense of propriety...

REASON #32: Becoming a monster of decorum, an Orthodox Jew of corporate kosher.

...but, for once, my curiosity outweighed my training as I found myself inching closer to Carlota and the end of the bed.

There, mostly covered by a sheet was my temptress, the glorious Eve, so still that my first response was terror. "Is she okay?" I whispered.

Carlota laughed. "Sleeping."

Eve was on her side, the sheet under her arm. As far as I could tell, she was naked. Without looking up I told Carla, "Nobody could sleep through that laugh of yours."

In her normal loud voice she replied, "It's the magic of mother's little helper," and held up a prescription bottle, one of those red ones you get at Target.

Without knowing I'd done so, I had moved in for a better look at that one slender shoulder and a close-up of that face. I could tell she was dreaming from the movement of the muscles around her eyes.

"You aren't going to drool on her, are you?"

I straightened. When did I become so transparent? Such a third-rate pervert? "Just making sure she's alright."

"I bet you didn't see this coming."

That's when it hit me. Carlota had told me when she'd met me at the door to the suite that she had a surprise for me. This was for me? Impossible. Unless Eve confided to Carlota some interest in me and the two had arranged this miraculous rendezvous. Were we to be two lovers brought together in a magical hotel room, presided over by a large cupid wearing Egyptian cotton?

Carlota moved to the other side of the bed, across from me, with Eve between us. She took hold of the edge of the sheet and said, "You want a peek?"

Oh, did I! But did I dare to eat that peach? She was an employee, and not at my level. I found myself croaking to Carlota, "It would be wrong," spoken with so little conviction that I must have sounded like Richard Nixon muttering into his lamp. Besides, wouldn't it be better to wait for Carlota to leave and for Eve to reveal herself by herself?

Carlota went ahead with the unveiling anyway, bless her. She slipped down the sheet and there was Eve, wearing surprisingly large black panties, but nothing else, her breasts alert and ready to sing Broadway tunes. I pretended to turn away, but made certain that my line of sight remained so I could mentally photograph each inch.

Such was the heat of imagination that I believed that if only Carlota would leave and I could awaken Eve with a kiss, then we could begin a proper romance. (Listen to me! A proper romance? Proper? Me, the Senior VP of HR in a hotel room, on a company trip, seducing a woman three levels below him? But there I was, yearning for Carlota to get out of the way and to let my inner beast take over as I ravaged this sweet innocent woman. I wished Putin could see me!)

But as impatient as I was to get on with it, I couldn't be angry with my terrycloth cupid. Somehow she had put this together for me. When I thought of all my thankless years at Mundane Industries, the chintzy bonuses, the occasional bulimic Thanksgiving turkey or the insult of a Dunkin' Donuts discount card, all was made up for by this, the ultimate employee benefit. I only wish I could call the author of the book *1,001 Ways To Reward Employees* and tell him to devote #1,002 to this one.

Carlota pulled the sheet back up. "That's all you get."

"This is so wrong, but so right. I don't know how you pulled this off, but thank you, thank you, thank you."

"Christ, you've never seen boobies before?"

"No, I mean arranging this rendezvous."

She laughed... too hard... a laugh with a bass note of cruelty. "You really are an idiot, Cheeseley. You think I brought her here for a three-way with you? Not a chance. She's all mine and she's worn out from two hours of lovemaking with me. My jaw is going to be sore for two days, not to mention... Christ, look at you. You look so heartbroken."

Yes, I was heartbroken, and yes, I was an idiot.

She came around the bed and reached out and took my right hand in her left, then reached up and flicked one of my nipples with a fingernail. "Don't worry. There's enough of me for both of you. But not together, you perv. And not tonight."

She reached up and turned my face to hers. "Don't be a puppy about it." She let the hand that had turned my head slide down and cup the bulge in my pants.

"I hate to waste another good boner, but after she's gone, then..." That busy hand of hers walked up my chest and back to my chin, which she gave a little shake, then slipped an index finger into my mouth. "Then you'll get your chance to be sore." She kissed me, full mouth, with her finger still in there, and I could just see Eve on the bed, who turned over and made a little moue and sighed, and I felt the full punch of what it means to be *that close*. Gatsby and his green light had nothing on me. Nothing. Oh, nothing.

Like Winning the Sack Race

I WENT TO MY BEDROOM on the other side of the living room, and while it might have been splendid to anyone else, I might as well have been in a 23 buck fly-strip of a room.

What was I to make of what had just transpired? Sure, there was the obvious fact that Carlota was a switch hitter. Fine. But Eve? When she came to my office to ask about dating a senior employee, she must have been thinking of Carlota. And there was the time in Genghis' office when she mentioned the photo and how she thought Carlota and I were dating... which, technically, was true as we were about to go on a second date. But she went with Carlota anyway. What did that tell me? Was she only attracted to women? To older women? Was she also attracted to men?

"She's attracted to power," said Putin, who must have slipped in while I was busy feeling sorry for myself. "Which is why you still have a chance, at least until she figures out that being Senior VP of HR has power status like winning the sack race at the company picnic."

I was still examining my mental photograph and let out a groan. "Did you see her in there? Now I know what I'm missing, and it's eating me up."

"Save the eating for tomorrow, for Carlota." He brayed at his little joke. Then, annoyed that I hadn't joined in, turned harsh. "Get over it. Slip in there now and kiss Eve on the lips and get a first taste of Carlota. That will help you realize that sex is sex. You have a song in your country... the one about love the one you're with. You're with Carlota."

"No. I can't be with Carlota. And Carlota can't be here with another employee, and I certainly can't know it. That makes me an accessory. I don't know if you know anything about lawsuits in this country, but Eve can sue the company. Imagine how it would look that she's sleeping with one executive while the head of HR is in the next room. Can you picture that?"

"You pay a bribe, you move on."

"That's not how it works over here."

"That's how it works everywhere. If you can buy a solution, it's not a problem; it's a negotiation. Quit worrying and start planning how to make the most of this situation. If she's already slept with one VP, what's another one? It's what you call a free-fer, no?"

"Either a freebie or a *two*-fer."

"So go now, while the situation is... lubricated. The two are both in there, in the bed. That's where you belong."

"I belong with Eve. If I go in there, it'll be with Carlota."

"It's dark. You call in a drone strike and it hits innocent civilian. So sorry."

"That's your advice? Go in there and tell Carlota that I can't wait till tomorrow, that I have to have her right now, and then, as I start to climb on top—oops!—I miss my target and stick my pecker into the woman sleeping next to her? That's your solution?"

"Start with where you want to finish and let the rest take care of itself."

"No. I can't do that. Not a chance."

He turned and went into the bathroom and came out, tossing a small plastic bottle to me. "It's hand lotion. Go crazy." And he was gone.

Maybe he was right. I could go in there and tell Carlota I had to have her. She'd believe me. And then we could get Eve involved. I pictured it in my mind, doing a visualization. I could see myself slipping in there and whispering to Carlota as I looked at Eve. I'd say to one ear what I longed to say to the ear a foot away. And then... oh, no... and then Carlota would say, "Okay, you horny thing, let's go in your room." And I would say... well... what?... I couldn't visualize anything past that.

You've Closed Off
A Lot of Options

I BROODED FOR A WHILE and concluded that I needed advice. I couldn't turn to relatives and certainly not to anyone at the office, not even Reggie. I needed someone with HR wisdom, but this was no topic to share with colleagues... except for one. The perfect person would be my Mad Joan, the woman I'd met and slept with at the conference. She knew how to keep a secret.

I had her cell number from that day in San Diego when she'd introduced me to the Senator. I checked my watch—9:30, her time. Late, but not that late. What would it hurt to try?

She didn't answer, so I left a message and she called back a minute later. The senator was out campaigning, and she was alone, drinking wine. Perfect. I swore her to secrecy and told her the problem, or half of it: "The daughter of the CEO, a fellow VP, wants to sleep with me. I have no interest in her, but can't afford to have her as an enemy, not when there's talk of outsourcing my department. We're here at the Bellagio, in separate rooms, but she's told me that tomorrow will be my lucky day? How do I decline?"

She pretended to take offense. "You're stuck with an unappealing woman, and you thought of me. That's just the ego boost I need."

"I thought of you because you're a sexy woman, and I'm

sure you've had dozens of men who wanted to sleep with you and who you turned down. And I'll bet you learned how to do it gracefully."

"Hmmm. I've always been better at yes than no. But, I do know how to do it. Ready?"

"I'll take notes."

"You say you just got your period."

"Great. Thanks. Don't tell me that's your only trick."

"Well, the problem is that you're in the hotel room. You don't want to get yourself into the hotel room and then say no. You've closed off a lot of options by that point."

"I can see that."

"Let me think. There was this one time. I changed my mind and didn't want to say so. I told the guy I was feeling a bit queasy and then went in the bathroom and filled the drinking cups with water and held them as high as I could then poured them into the toilet. And I moaned as I did. Then I told him I had diarrhea but was willing to go on with the sex. I thought that would end things, but he leaned in for a kiss...men!... so I puffed out my cheeks like I was going to vomit and ran back to the restroom and did more loud water. I stayed in there a long time. My next move was going to be to ask if I could use his toothbrush, just to test him and see where he was on the horniness index, but he was asleep and I slipped out."

"Good lord, you are a devious one."

"I have my gifts."

"Is that the best you've got?"

She thought for a moment. "There's being gay."

"Too much evidence to the contrary has already been put forward."

"Herpes?"

"There's a great rumor to have following me forever."

"Well, you could just close your eyes and think of

England. Or, instead of England, you could think of me. That could even be a turn on, if you thought about it the right way."

"You've got me curious. What would be the right way to think about it?"

"In my case, to the hum of a vibrator."

"It'll be a blue, blue Christmas without you."

Rather Like a Good First Lady

THE NEXT MORNING I sat in bed straining to hear if my roommates were up. Nothing. Perhaps they were sleeping in. I hoped so, for I longed for the chance to snap some mental photographs of Eve awakening, Eve in nightdress, Eve at breakfast. That way I'd have a set of memories to save for... well, to help me make a decision about whether or not to continue my pursuit of her affections. I was of two minds about that, or maybe just two body parts.

Anyway, I slipped into the living room of the suite and saw no evidence of anyone having gotten up. As it was just an hour till our meeting with the investors, I felt justified in being the human alarm clock for the pair of them. I stepped in, casting off normal courtesies, hoping for peeks, knocking as I went. But all I peeked was rumpled bedding. There was no one in there and just a few items of clothing in the closet, their size making it clear they belonged to Carlota and not Eve.

When I called Carlota's cellphone, she was all business, firing off an instruction to show up early in the conference center of the hotel so we could "strategize."

I gladly did so, arriving early-early, hoping to have time to discuss with Carlota the evening before, but she arrived late-early and she arrived in her office persona, informing me that the strategy for the meeting amounted to my shutting up and letting her do the negotiating. "Just remember, you're here to play the part of my fiancé, so act adoring and supportive. Then once the negotiations begin, treat their every offer as a disappointment." Before I could change the subject, the other side arrived and we were swept into the negotiation.

It was my assignment to act adoring and supportive— rather like a good First Lady—so that came easily, as did looking pained at the offers.

I won't go into the whole meeting, but we were with four Arab businessmen, three fidgety loquacious young men in suits and sandals, and one older one, also in a suit, but in loafers and who said nothing, sitting motionless like a lizard basking.

There was a bit of the usual small talk about who'd won and lost at the tables the night before and what the city and hotel had to offer. What I should have prepared myself for were the congratulations of the young Arabs. I'd forgotten the cover story about getting "engaged" and that I was meant to be the swooning swain, so when one said, "That's quite a rock you got your lady," I was befuddled and could only manage "Rock?"

"My English isn't perfect," he said, "but I did go to school at Columbia and MIT, and I was under the impression that the stone on an engagement ring was known as a rock. Am I mistaken?"

Carlota then proudly extended to the group a hand with rings on three fingers and I had to count off mentally to see the one he meant. Not blinding, but much more impressive than anything I would have actually purchased.

Having seen the "rock" and having muttered approval, all four dark faces, plus Carlota's, turned to hear my comment. But what do you say about a ring you've never seen, much less purchased? You'd think Carlota would have bothered to tell me about this chapter in the story of our imaginary engagement. Still, a Cheeseley loves a challenge and I came through and can't help but feel some pride at this bit of magic: "This has all been such a whirlwind. I have to keep asking myself if it's really true."

The four Arabs looked at me with disbelief, and at least one of them must have been feeling a keen relief that he had, after all, not been set up with Carlota for an arranged romance.

They moved on to the business of day. None of the issues meant much to me, mostly squabbling about cost calculations and logistics, and I found myself studying Carlota as she worked.

She was dressed in the femi-diplomat style, out on the Angela Merkel/Hillary Clinton end of the continuum. The power-look suited her, and she worked her side of the negotiations skillfully, using anecdotes and appeals to masculinity to hide her merciless refusal to compromise, winning them with the relentless cheeriness of the mass murderer who charms his way into your house. I'd seen Genghis himself in action many times; she was better.

On three occasions Carlota leaned over to whisper to me, but this was just for show. She was buying time by pretending to consult with me. I did my part, patting her arm while sighing at the Arabs and sadly shaking my head, even as, on one of the occasions, she whispered, "I wish they'd hurry up and cave, because these pantyhose are pinching my ass."

Near the end, she offered up a small concession to provide them an excuse to concede. As she later told me, a victor philosophizing, "You take all the hundred dollar bills on the table but leave behind one dime and eventually they end up telling themselves that it was the dime that really mattered all along. Do it right, and they believe they actually won."

She made arrangements for us to meet the Arabs for

dinner to celebrate the new business relationship, and as we walked off, she told me that she was going to meet a friend and that she'd see me that evening at the restaurant.

"Could we talk for a minute before you go?"

"Talk?"

"About what happened last night."

"Nothing happened."

"Carlota, as head of HR, I have responsibilities..."

"Shut it, Win. Responsibilities, my ass. Nothing happened last night except your drinking too much and falling asleep and talking in your sleep about Eve and generally embarrassing yourself. I'm trying to forget it and I expect you to let me."

So there it was, the deny-everything strategy, which, by the way, is one I would recommend to you whenever you're in a jam over any sort of tawdry behavior. Don't even let the discussion start; an explanation is an admission. On the other hand, the denial allows you to look dignified while forcing the other side to get down on their knees to look for stains.

The truth was that Carlota had just given me a pass to the charmed state of plausible deniability. What had I done? Gone to a hotel room and gone to sleep. Alone. Eve had not seen me. No one had, but Carlota, who was insisting I was talking in my sleep. So there were just those few minutes between walking in and lying down that had given me a series of unforgettable images that I could easily not recall. Carlota was giving me an out.

I sighed and from somewhere came a line, maybe Shakespeare or maybe from the old "I Dream of Jeannie" TV show: "I have had the most rare vision. I have had a dream past the wit of man to say what dream it was."

She gave me a quarter-smile and moved in tight, startling me with a half-hearted crotch grab that made me yelp. "Till later," she cooed, and departed.

So I had for myself an afternoon in Vegas, which sounds like it could be a movie title. Right. My afternoon held no romance and no adventure, just HR. When you're in HR, your work pursues you like Dog the Bounty Hunter and ruthlessly pins you to a tastefully upholstered chair in the hallway of the conference wing of the hotel. You always have to be available, just in case this one time it really is an emergency, like a great employee threatening to leave or a potential lawsuit or a whacked-out ex-employee with a gun and nothing left to lose.

REASON #33: Being in HR and being issued a corporate cellphone is not much different than being issued a court-ordered GPS ankle bracelet. They can always find you.

Let me give you two highlights of my afternoon, just so you'll know how An Afternoon in Vegas becomes, inexorably, Just Another Afternoon on the Phone, which is the name you can give to the movie of your career if you continue in your misguided plans. I checked my phone and found 14 voicemail messages and 34 new emails. I pass along only the Best Of...

First there was a sniveling voicemail from FullOfHimself, who'd had a young woman come to him to complain about Mitch "Bama" Biggs, one of our VPs, who'd recently taken to referring to her as "Sugar" and "Honey." I knew the woman in question, and to be candid, "Prickly" and "Standoffish" would have been more accurate, and perhaps those would be less offensive to her as she felt "belittled" by Bama's generous labels.

FullOfHimself had called me in an attempt to edge out of taking on a VP of Bama's stature, and in normal circumstances I would have done my young charge the favor of declining. (When a manager takes over for an employee, the employee is grateful but enfeebled.)

However, seeing as how I was miffed at FullOfHimself for overreaching with Genghis, I decided to just call Bama myself. After all, this sweetness talk was not just a familiar problem; it was an annual one.

I called and quickly brought him round to the point. "Bama, let me guess—you've just been vacationing back home in Anniston."

"Oh good God yes. If I try real hard, I can still smell the magnolias."

"And every year you come back, and I get a call from someone in your division and…"

"Winslow, I swear on my mama's pee-can pie, I have been an angel boy. Let me tell you, I haven't given anyone a shoulder massage in four years, even though every day I see shoulders yearning for a bit of comfortin'. And, hell, I haven't gotten myself a shoulder massage in two years, at least not in the office. I still don't understand how anyone could bitch… er, gripe… about a shoulder massage, but that's this new world. I guess these Millennials just send a text message and say BREATHE and that's all they need. But what about my feelings? My needs?"

I was smiling and I knew he was, too; we both loved to hear him talk. "You know that I care about your feelings," I began, "and your needs. Why? Because Mundane Industries needs you, Bama. We love you. And, hey, good work on keeping hands off shoulders. It's not that. It's someone getting bothered by you calling them Honey and Sugar."

"Well, when you say it, it sounds like a brand of cereal. When I say it, people smile and want to hug me, and then if it was up to you, I'd have to hide under my desk for fear you'll be callin' me about gettin' hugs. What sort of fool could object to Honey or Sugar?"

"Maybe it was the same sort who complained last year about Sweetie and Dearheart."

"Win, Win, Win. How the world disappoints this ole country boy. And the world discriminates agin him, too. It's discriminatin' against Southerners. Everybody else has pet names for employees and nobody cares, but let a Southerner say boo and suddenly you're a bigot or a sexite or sumthin."

He meant sexist, of course, but I let it go. "You might be right." (There is one of the worlds' most useful phrases: You might be right.) "But here's the thing. The problem is using language that could be seen to diminish someone. Not everyone is as self-confident as you. So we have to be sensitive to the needs of the sensitive."

"You know me, Win, a team player. All I'm asking for is fairness."

REASON # 34: Fairness.

I tried to change the subject: "If life were fair, you and I would have bought Microsoft stock in 1980." That made no sense, and I don't know when you should have bought Microsoft, but it was the best I could do on the fly.

"I'll make you a deal. I'll stop calling people Sugar. Just as soon as James stops calling everyone Kiddo. Or Camilla, who, ever since she worked on John McCain's campaign, calls everyone My Friend. She has no friends, and yet nobody is hasslin' her over her My Friend. And there's whatshisname who calls everybody Dude, and Lamar who calls everyone Bro, even the women. How many of these do you need before you stop me and say, 'You are so right, Dear Bama. I apologize for doubtin' ya-all.'?"

I gave him a bit of massage oil for the soul. "I'm glad I don't have to debate you. You would have been a better Presidential candidate than John McCain."

"I've had inquiries about running for Congress, but this gerbil ain't gonna volunteer to go running up inside Washington's... Well, let me stop myself 'fore I get too colorful for the sensitive souls that might overhear me."

I wondered whether FullOfHimself would have gotten the full gerbil analogy, but I just kept moving him around to my side. "Well. Getting back to the point. You can use a general term for your employees but only if you use it with everyone, and by everyone I mean young and old, male and female."

"Therefore, so as long as I start calling the guys Sugar, then I am fine by you?"

"At least until one of the guys thinks you're insulting him or maybe coming on to him." Back to the oil, I added, "You're too valuable to be risking your career over silly stuff like this."

He harrumphed, and I knew he had turned the corner. I invited him to come the rest of the way. "I know it seems beneath worrying about, but my job is to worry about everyone getting along. Don't make me worry. Do it for me."

"Dammit, Win, I can't say no to you... Sugarpie."

We laughed, and I knew he'd come around and there it was, the Sugar and Honey crisis averted, at least till his next vacation back home.

The next problem was a measure of how far we've come in gender equality. Years ago it was a common assignment for anyone in HR to tell the guys in the warehouse to take down the *Playboy* centerfold pinned to the wall, or the latest swimsuit model calendar from some tool company. That almost never happens anymore. This time the problem was a female employee in the warehouse who'd put on her desk a photo of her and her husband at the beach, both wearing bikinis. I called and, after being cheery, got to the point.

"Sherrie, you know I hate to get involved in personal items at the office, but I've had a report of a provocative phone on your desk." Yes, I said *phone*. Confusion is your friend.

"A provocative phone?"

"Did I say phone? I meant photo. I'm losing my mind. I think they said it was a beach photo. Does that make any sense?" Now I'm the one confused and she's going to help me.

"I put out a new picture from San Diego."

"That could be it. Could someone find it... you know, too... too... revealing. Like I say, I haven't seen it."

She laughed. "I'm looking pretty hot or I wouldn't have put it on my desk."

"I don't doubt that." (There's another golden phrase, right up there under "You could be right.") "But somebody must think it's *too* hot." What I wasn't saying was that the complaint was about her husband's bikini, not hers. "We don't want to distract the other employees, do we?"

"I don't know. It's pretty lonely out here after the last layoffs. I could use some people coming by to visit."

"I know what you mean." (There it is, the third of the agreeableness troika, right after "I don't doubt that" and "You could be right")

I eased us back to the issue. "This makes no sense to me, but somebody must have been concerned by the photo. You know how people are. Do you have any pictures of say, the San Diego Zoo?"

"I did get a good one of a baby giraffe."

"That would make my day. I'll come by tomorrow and see that baby giraffe."

Notice that I'd slipped in a deadline for the new photo and a warning that I'd be checking up, all by way of being everybody's friend, Mr. Happy.

Crisis two, averted.

The rest of the afternoon was like that. I'd listen to voicemail, get on the phone and sweet talk or cajole my way to a win-win solution, then read my email and do more of the same, and by the time I had finished with email, my voicemail had lined up more problems. It was like looking out at the night sky and seeing the lights of the planes in the landing pattern for the airport—you could count them but you did so knowing that they were countless.

My Honeymoon

THEN THERE WAS DINNER. We all met at a restaurant that was fabulous and yet so conventional in its wonderfulness that I don't recall the name. We spent an hour on the topic of why Carlota and I should visit Dubai, especially for our honeymoon, and while I passed myself off as intrigued, I was distracted by the "honeymoon" I would face that very evening. There we'd be in a Bellagio suite, the city spread before us, a bedroom on either side of us, and I had to make a decision that might affect my entire future. This would be what we call in business a pivot point.

I told myself that I must steel myself to be candid. I would just come out and tell Carlota that my job would no longer include pretending to be her lover. There would be no sex, and that was that. If that offended her, and she turned on me and encouraged her father to hire Wiseman & Regary to take over my department and they fired me, well, so be it.

So be it. That sounded big and bold. So be it. Above it all. But what was the "it" waiting up there, above it all? The likelihood that I'd never again get a Director's job. Come to think of it, being an older white male who might end up walking away carrying sexual harassment allegations, maybe I'd never work again. So be it. Maybe after a year of unemployment I'd be forced to move into a two-bedroom apartment with a roommate who ate Cheetos while cheering on Judge Judy, and I'd end up taking a job in fast food, perhaps as a Sandwich Artist, cheerfully asking, "All the fixin's?"

So... no. No so. No be it. After a couple of hours with such reflections, and after a couple of excellent margaritas, I began to reconsider. I actually found myself humming under my breath Fagin's song from *Oliver* about reviewing the situation and it must have gotten up over my breath because Carlota gave me a kick to the shin that left a lump.

What was so bad about being a kind of corporate gigolo? I'd play my part with Carlota while thinking of England or my Mad Joan or Salma Hayek, for that matter. The only real question was, Could I maintain concentration, by which I mean a hard-on? We Cheeseleys are men of steel. I could do it. Probably.

I needed Putin to coach me and I looked around the room and saw him at the bar with a woman you would knock down Salma Hayek to get your hands on. I caught his eye, and he held up a champagne flute in salutation, but when I signaled him to go to the Men's room, he made a shooing gesture then leaned in and kissed the woman. So there it was: I was destined to spend a night in a Bellagio suite with Carlota and a big probably.

An hour later we were back there, in the suite. Carlota asked if I wanted a drink, and I declined, wanting to avoid any diffusing of my mental and physical steeling.

"Get me one," she instructed. There was a bar in the room, and I started to warn her about the cost implications of breaking the seal on the vodka, but stopped myself. Tonight, corporate expenses be damned. (Christ, I can't believe I thought that.) I felt myself getting taller and I realized I was finding my inner Putin.

She was sitting on the sofa so I sat there, too. Not too

far away, but not rubbing up against her. She flipped off her heels and put up her legs, her feet in my lap. I have always found the feel of nylons erotic, so I willingly started in massaging. I found myself disappearing into the role of Putin, and weirdly, I began to think of Sarah Palin. Of all the women on the planet, I thought of Sarah Palin? Good God, I just don't know anything anymore. Still, it was working, and I was stiffening beneath her black stockings.

That's when the feet were jerked away and Carlota stood to drop her skirt and pull down and off her pantyhose, thus releasing a hillock of cellulite that would be a profound test for any erotic imagination.

"That's better," she announced and resumed her position with her feet in my lap. She poked at my manhood and said, "It doesn't take you long, you horny perv."

What she didn't know is that the plug had been pulled, and I was entering deflation mode. I needed to get us into the bedroom where it was darker and I had more options for where to not look.

"There must be other places where you're holding tension," I said, trying to make it sound sexy but feeling it came off as medical advice. "Maybe we should lie down in the other room."

She gave me a look I couldn't quite decode, perhaps she had picked up on the Putin spirit that had entered into me and was a bit intimidated.

We went in the bedroom, hers, and as I took off my shirt and shoes she pulled off her blouse and lay face down in her bra and panties—black lace trim, expensive looking, and hooboy large. But the Putin-spirit and I weren't criticizing, just accepting, although Sarah Palin was long gone and I was struggling to find a mental image I could sell to the customer inside my shorts. I hit upon the image of Kirstie Alley, and it wasn't long before that worked. I began massaging her shoulders and worked my way down as my member pumped its way back up, slowly achieving an acceptable firmness and I debated whether it was time to slip off my trousers.

Problem. As I was decided on timing I'd worked my way down her back to where I encountered a section of lower back skin that seemed to have crumbs stuck to it. I tried to brush them away, but realized they were not only stuck, but living flesh, those little things called skin tags, like vertical warts, making it feel like I was running my hands over stubble... meat stubble.

This caused me to once again lose emotional and physical altitude; I hand-jumped down to the black silk panties and begged Kirstie to come back into this fantasy. Kirstie wasn't that picky, apparently; she returned. I could feel Carlota starting to respond to the work of my hands and biology took over and there it was, the scent of a woman. Would that be enough?

That's when I heard someone in the living room. I assumed it was the maid, come to do the silly turn-down service and leave a mint. But no, it was a woman and a man. Carlota sat up and said merrily, "Daddy's here."

Daddy? Genghis? Here?

She handed me my shirt and said, "Go keep him company while I get dressed."

I tried to decline, but she shoved me toward the bedroom door, which we hadn't bothered to close. I took a step and there he was, along with Mrs. Cone, groping for the light switch.

"How nice to see you," I lied, just as the light came on.

"Cheeseley?" he asked, annoyed, without a hint of embarrassment at having walked in on a man with no shirt but, with pants and, thanks to my earlier deflation, a soft-on. He was filling up the doorway and did have the decency to instruct his wife to wait outside the bedroom door. He gestured toward my bare chest and added, "This... this relationship with Carlota is a story for investors. I don't want you touching her."

I thought of the meat stubble and felt ready to take the pledge, but having become one with Putin, I found myself saying, "Who knows with passion? Who can tell a fire not to burn?"

"Anyone with a hose."

But before the evening could turn into a clash of wills, Carlota appeared out of the bathroom and hugged her father and began talking of her triumphs with the Arab businessmen, and once dollars were being discussed, the two of them forgot me.

But not Mrs. Cone, who was exploring the suite and established herself and her husband in the other bedroom; that is, in my bedroom. That's when Carlota called Eve and gave her orders to find a room for me. Back to the Golden Somethingorother. (Twenty-eight dollars this time. Short notice.)

As I was leaving the splendor of the room at the Bellagio, Carlota stepped into the hall and tenderly fondled my crotch. "Poor little fiancé. You may have to wait till our wedding night."

Wedding night?

She slipped just the tip of her steamy cat tongue between my frozen lips then turned her head one way and another before she slipped back inside the suite. I could just make out her saying "unit costs" before the door clunked shut.

Wedding night?

A joke, surely, but where was the laugh? Where was the laugh?

Without Asking,
He Shut My Door

IT WAS EARLY AFTERNOON before I got back to Phoenix and the office. Just as I reached for the phone to check in with Reggie, the head of our R&D department, Keith Cushing, came bustling into my office. Without asking, he shut my door and dragged a visitor's chair in close to my desk.

He was fuming and didn't hesitate to explain why. One of his employees, our most talented engineer, a young woman of Asian descent, had just told him that he was "full of shit." He hotly responded that he'd have her fired for insubordination. However, being a committed bureaucrat, he hadn't thrown her out. Instead, he informed her that she'd be gone just as soon as he could complete the paperwork. He was in my office to ask how to jump the usual warning process and go right to firing her.

There were two problems, and neither one involved justifying an immediate firing. Problem one was that he was indeed full of shit. Problem two was that she was the best we had, a genius at her job, and more important to the company than her boss.

Backing up, you might wonder why a manufacturer of me-too products would have an R&D department. There is an art to the speedy imitation of others' products. There's the underrated skill of reverse engineering, the process whereby you take a finished product and figure out how it had been made and how it could be duplicated. But more rare is the skill of finding a way to make a similar product without violating the inevitable patents. Thus, you have to find a different way to do what they have done. This was where Momoko entered in. (Great name, no? Some people call her Momo and some Moke and some Moko, but all do so with affection.) Instead of just figuring out some acceptable reconfiguration, she routinely hit upon a superior method. Mundane Industries had been able to patent a number of her processes and then sell these to the very companies whose products inspired them.

All of that was beyond the business model or human resources strategy of Mundane Industries. The truth was that she was too good to be working for us. She was, in marketing parlance, a premium brand, and we don't pay retail, much less premium. We could afford her only because her husband had been brought to town to work on a major biomedical research project and she hadn't wanted to split the family.

If she was so talented, why not make her head of R&D? She didn't want the job, and even if she had, I knew her husband would be transferred back to the San Francisco area in a year or two and she would follow.

REASON # 35: Keeper of the Myths. (In this case, the myth that every member of the team is important and should all be treated equally.)

This was a crisis worthy of all the skills that had earned me my nickname Win-Win. As Keith spoke, detailing the accusations against her, I went deep into myself, summoning up all my reserves of agreeableness. I even said an HR Prayer: "Please, God—or Goddess or Earth Mother or Higher Power or Universal Life Force or any of the other names that I have forgotten but do not mean to exclude,

including a Never Mind for our nonbelievers—give me
the wisdom and skill to outsmart and out-negotiate my
employees, for their own good."

I held back and let him tell the full story, which was
that the two had disagreed and he'd pulled rank and
she reached the conclusion that he was wrong, or, in a
moment of understandable pique, that he was full of shit.
The sticky side was that the insult had been overheard
by two other staffers. His conclusion: "She's got to go
and now. No options. My authority has been called into
question, and I can't run this department if people are
sniggering behind my back."

Here's the genius of a skilled HR professional: Keep
agreeing with them until they agree with you. That's why
I made sympathetic noises until he finished.

Key word: finished. If you are patient, there comes a
moment when the anger has been fully discharged, as
though indignation were battery powered. I jumped in,
softly, inserting reassurance. "I understand and I'm with
you. Let's think through how to do this right."

"I need to come out of this stronger in the eyes of my
team. Jack Welch once looked me straight in the eye and
told me, 'Control your own destiny or someone else will.'"

Keith had spent a few years at GE when Welch was
running things and had a Welch quote for every occasion. From what I'd learned about him, the bit about the
head of GE looking him straight in the eye was a wild
exaggeration, unless you counted the giant eyes on the
big projection screens when the CEO lectured thousands
at corporate events.

I agreed, of course. "Absolutely. Let's think about your
destiny. Or maybe I should say all your possible destinies,
because we all know that we are shaped by the people we
are shaping. Momoko has blossomed under your guid-

ance, and you have made her a star. That's part of your destiny, to create stars. Nobody has more of a reputation for mentoring and bringing along talent than you do, and Exhibit A has been Ms. Moko. "

Was this remotely true? Let's just say that he believed it.

He replied, "I don't know what you're trying to say to me except that yes, I helped her become a star and she can get a job in a minute so I'm not going to worry about her. I need to worry about the team and keeping their respect."

"Exactly." That's not at all where I was going, but remember: Agree with them till they agree with you. "She's not the issue. The team is. And you've made her into the star of the team. That's your destiny. You're the Phil Jackson of corporate coaches, and she's your Michael Jordan. I want to help you figure out how to not let her play for the other team. That would be like you working against yourself, and who wins that?"

You see how I'm moving him around to the other side of the negotiation table, to the side I'm sitting on. He might not agree that she was better than he was, but if he saw her genius as coming from him, then he'd have to be daunted by the competition.

"Well, I hope you have a good non-compete agreement in her contract. But even if you don't, as Jack Welch once told me, 'You have to be willing to change, even if it means plunging into chaos.'"

"But he also said, 'You don't have to love everyone you work with, just love the talent they bring to the job.'" I made that up and, hey, I think it's better than the BS Welch tosses around. I added, "What would Welch do if his star player made a mistake and then felt just terrible about it—would he give that star a chance to apologize and to keep helping the team?"

"I doubt it. And she did *not* apologize. She may have

even tried to flip me the bird. She held up her little finger, and I think she thought she was flipping me off."

"Keith. I can't reveal my sources on this so don't ask, but my insider scoop is that she was in tears, heartsick that she'd let down the man she respected so much." The source of this inside intelligence? My imagination.

"Ha. Really?"

"She wants to make it up to you. And the way to do that is to continue to be your star player. You don't want to be the one who let Michael Jordan go because of a momentary flare-up. What I'm asking myself is this: Is Keith Cushing a big enough man to let an insult go? And the answer I'm believing for is *yes*, Keith Cushing is big enough."

Silence. I knew he was weighing the possibility that he might be thought of as the idiot who fired Michael Jordan. "She was crying over letting me down?"

"She's too vain to let you see it, but if I know her real feelings, she wants to beg you to forgive her. So why don't I call her and issue an official reprimand and let her get back to working for the man who's made her what she is?"

"I can't let anybody get away with talking to me like that."

"And you didn't. I'll get on the reprimand right now. And I'll tell her she owes you. It's a fine, big thing you're doing."

He muttered and grumbled, but it was just show, as was my pretense that the crisis had just been averted. I still had to persuade Momoko to stay in her job and to refrain from future outbursts. While I could do that, I doubted that I could convince her to apologize or demonstrate contrition. So I had to prepare him for an unapologetic employee to return the next morning.

"One thing to remember, Keith: the Asian culture. They can't lose face. They don't publicly climb down. Just coming back to work is an admission that she was wrong. It's her apology. I hope you'll accept it and move on. Phil Jackson would. Jack Welch would. And Keith Cushing?"

He pulled himself as if to have a medal pinned on. "Yes, Keith Cushing will too."

The art of persuasion is often the skillful editing and rewriting of events. You grow a better future by finding the right past to plant it in. Oh yeah, that last sentence was diamonds. Jack Welch wishes he could come up with lines like that.

YOU AREN'T CRAZY

IT WAS TIME FOR ANOTHER VISIT with Reggie. I am always pleased when we get to visit, even though he is the most intense man I know. It's as though he uses up all the seriousness in the room so everyone else can relax.

I decided to walk over to the hall where he had his office, and the two of us ended up going into one of the conference rooms. (The usual: a conference table of fake wood with eight fake leather chairs and overhead tubes buzzing with fake sunlight. This is one of the places where I lecture managers on the importance of authenticity.)

"I wanted to give you my report on my investigation," he began. "Executive summary: I don't like it. I've gone through my preliminary list and I can't find a single legitimate suspect. There are plenty of people who hate the economy and the company and even you, but I can't ID a single strong suspect. You're there in the hate vortex, but my gut tells me that no one I've looked at is capable of making it about you."

This was my exact conclusion after the focus group. "What's not to like about that?"

"There's that damn cartridge that was on your desk. I can't make it fit into any theory I've come up with—and I've come up with a hundred."

"So let's conclude that it was just an angry outburst, an ugly prank like the guy who took a dump on my desk or the woman who tried to smash my windshield with a brick and ended up with a broken hand. Just another ugly prank."

"You know me, Win. I don't quit. I don't give up. I just need some fresh lead, some new theory... something."

"You've been a real friend, Reggie. And this is a victory, not a defeat. This is good news. I can stop being paranoid. I still feel awful about dragging you over to my condo the other night."

He winked. Not many men, and no woman, can pull that off. Forget I said that, the part about no woman.

"Your neighbor and I," he told me in a dull voice, "are going to a gun show this weekend. In Albuquerque."

Although he'd said it as though scheduled for an IRS audit, I knew he'd enjoy himself. "I'm glad some good has come of it."

"But you aren't crazy. She confirmed the unusual activity of unfamiliar vehicles."

"Again, though, there's no logic in it. If someone wanted to beat me up, they'd have done it long ago. And who'd carjack my car? It's an okay car, but there are dozens of better ones right in the condo complex."

"Phoenix is the kidnapping capital of the country. And you are one of the highest ranking executives at one of the most profitable companies in the city."

"I'm in HR for Christ's sake. You kidnap the CEO or the engineer with the secret formula, not the HR guy. And nobody knows that we're a profitable company, and if they do, they know that Mr. Cone would never spend a penny on ransom."

Reggie almost smiled as he said, "It could become a profit center for him. Like *Ransom of Red Chief*."

(I'm not sure what they teach you in school these days, but I doubt it's the marvelous short story by O'Henry. It's about the kidnapping of a young boy. Trying to keep up with the little whirlwind is so exhausting that the kidnappers plead with the parents to take him back, eventually offering money for the relief of returning him.)

We had a good laugh over that, and I left feeling that my load was at least a bit lighter. I didn't have to look around in fear for my physical safety, at least if you didn't count Carlota.

Four-and-a-quarter hours later, I was kidnapped.

A Nun in a Wheelchair

CLEVER, THE WAY THEY PULLED IT OFF. Driving home, I was about to turn into the little side street that is the entrance to my condo community, a heavily landscaped lane where you wait for the gates to open. That's when I noticed a nun in a wheelchair crossing to the island where you punch in an entry code or dial-up a resident to open the gates. Naturally, I stopped to let her cross, and when her chair lurched to the side and she tumbled out, I leapt from my car to assist her. That's when a van pulled up to likewise give aid, or so I thought. Instead of me lifting the nun, she rolled onto her feet and grabbed me. With the help of a young tough, the two of them tossed me into the van. I looked back to my car and watched a third young brigand hop in and drive off. The nun, who turned out to be an athletic male with braces on his teeth, pulled the wheelchair onboard, and we were off.

This was no windowless child-molester van, this was the sort that second-rate hotels send to pick you up at the airport, a pair of bucket seats up front and three rows behind. I'd been tossed into the middle row and the phony nun had taken the row behind and the one who'd hoisted me effortlessly into the van sat in the row ahead of me. That accounted for all of us, except for the driver, who I'd only seen from behind and who seemed older and heavier than the other two.

How scared was I? Well, I didn't scream. And there was something about those braces on the teeth that made the event somehow civilized. Yes, I'd had a surge of adrenaline when I'd been yoicked off the ground and relocated into the van. But the two who'd taken me weren't particularly scary. They were young Hispanics, smiling and efficient, the sort I like to hire. They wore sunglasses and Pancho Villa fake moustaches as a primitive but effective disguise. The one sitting in the row in front half turned to me, showed me a handgun and said in a voice without accent or interest, "I hear you're a smart man, so let me give you the rules. In case you're feeling like running, you should know that the door next to you doesn't open from the inside. If you move, I'll shoot your knee and since we aren't about to take you to a hospital, you'd probably bleed to death. Now put these on." He handed me sunglasses, the wraparound kind, which was a sweet touch given the late afternoon glare, but as I obeyed I learned that the inside of the lenses had been painted black which turned them into a blindfold. Smart, right? I couldn't see anything and yet I didn't have a black hood or a towel wrapped around my head or anything else that would arouse suspicion.

The guy in the nun's habit reached over me, the cloth from the oversized sleeves kiting about, and clicked handcuffs onto me, mercifully in front, not behind my back.

Given that I'm a nervous person, a worrier, it was unlike me to be calm. Putin would be proud. Then again, I'd just discussed getting kidnapped a few hours before. It helped to know that I was in the hands of bored professionals. Just business. Nothing personal. How often we HR people say those words, and here I was, living them.

I had no idea where we were going and I couldn't identify any of the people who'd abducted me. This was a good thing, I reasoned, as it would increase my chances of being returned unharmed. That makes it sound like I have insider knowledge of criminal behavior, but what I know is based on reading detective fiction. Then again, I've read in journalists' accounts of actual crime that much of what criminals know is based on televised crime fiction.

Thinking things through, my concern was that my captors might turn vindictive when they learned that I had no monetary value as a hostage. That's when I remembered that in the world of kidnappers "just business" seemed to routinely include the sending of fingers or other body parts to those being hit up for money. I had no immediate family and none with access to serious money, and I knew Genghis wouldn't pay up even if they FedExed a pound of me a day for the twenty or thirty days or however long it would take to have cut the life out of me.

All of which distracted me from what I knew to be my assignment as a hostage, to count off the seconds to each turn as a way to one day help the police reconstruct the route. I was also diverted from my obligations by the fact that the sunglasses were missing the nose pad on one side and therefore sat ever so slightly askew, affording me a sliver of vision. If I moved my head like a camera panning, I could assemble an image. This wasn't of any practical value till we reached our destination and stopped, allowing me to do a slow pan and see that we were pulling into a typical suburban house, stucco, newish, probably built during the great real estate boom. That fit with the fact that we'd been driving for a while so I figured we were in one of the distant suburbs.

The van pulled into the garage, and we all sat while the electric door mumbled shut behind us.

The man in front of me pulled the sunglasses off my face and announced, "Welcome to your new home." He then opened my door—from the inside, the liar—and I stepped into the garage. They hadn't done anything with it, none of the little features that make the suburban garage special, like the epoxy paint on the floor or built-in cabinets along the walls.

The garage door led into the kitchen and there were two women cooking something that smelled wonderful. I was so calm that I took time to speculate they were cooking the old-fashioned way, with lard. However, the women didn't look up, and my little posse wasn't stopping for a taste test.

We turned a corner, and that's when I saw, heard and smelled them: the dozens of people packed into the house. It was immediately clear to me that they were illegals from Mexico or beyond and that this was a waypoint on their journey to a new life in America. Many of them looked away, but others were curious. Perhaps I was the first Anglo they'd seen in their new country and some of them smiled and a few even greeted me, one kid trying out his English and saying, "Good afternoon, Old Sport." Perhaps he'd seen *The Great Gatsby* movie.

You can't have lived in Arizona for a decade and not have developed an affection for Latinos. I know you've heard the crap in the news about how Arizona hates illegals, and I suppose that some citizens resent the drag on government services, but spend some time with Hispanics and you come to love them. Yes, okay, I'm generalizing and I know there are hard-hearted gang members roaming about somewhere. But the Latinos I've known are, without exception, fun-loving people, with a passion for music and family and who share the same God and the love of liberty and the American Dream. When it comes to the last of these, they also possess a dogged willingness to work for it that is missing from so many American-born employees.

(My previous employer, prior to the tight-fisted Genghis Cone, had decided to undertake a program to help

Hispanic employees go back to school. Despite the generous tuition reimbursement plan that I devised, almost
no one took us up on the offer. When I'd asked why, the
immigrants told me that they had it made; in fact, they
had literally made it... to America, that is... then gotten
legal status and gotten a house and car and they were *satisfied*. Why go to college if you'd made it? What American
born here, deposited straight from the womb into the
American Dream, would ever smile and say, "No, thank
you, I'm *satisfied*"?)

So you won't be surprised to hear that as I looked at
all the brown faces I smiled and waved in greeting as best
as I could with the handcuffs still in place. As I waved I
could feel the crowd relaxing. No immigration officer
would show up in handcuffs.

There was an old television in the family room and a
few plastic lawn chairs, but otherwise no furniture. The
residents stood or sat on the carpeted floor.

I was taken to the farthest of four bedrooms. As I
would soon learn, that last bedroom was the only fur-
nished room, set up as an office. Seated at a desk was
the person in charge, and you can imagine my surprise
that the person was a woman, wearing sunglasses and
an Angels baseball cap over long wavy dark hair tucked
behind square ears. She was lighting a cigar, and though
I've never been a smoker, she maneuvered it with an assurance that made her seemed skilled at the task. Everyone
waited in silence, just like we'd all wait for Mr. Cone to
pull the mechanical pencil from his mouth and begin
the meeting.

Satisfied with her cigar, she gave me an inverted nod
and said, "I am El Papagayo."

That meant nothing to me but I later learned that
"papagayo" is "parrot" and that the cap hid the red spike

of hair that prompted the nickname. (If you have any Spanish you may wonder why it was El Papagayo and not La Papagaya. I assumed that she wanted to overcome sexism when dealing with those she didn't meet in person, but later decided that she was flaunting the notion of machismo, like those scary women who boast about their "balls.")

She wore no makeup but had a complexion that didn't need help. Her movements were loose, like an athlete before age and injury knot up the sinews. It was obvious within the first sentences that English was not her first language. Still, her English was largely free from mispronunciations. Perhaps a real nun had whacked English into her. If so, that nun would probably give her an A-minus because she had a couple of old habits unbroken, ones I would come to enjoy. There was the "j" sound that took over for "y"—her "jes" for "yes" and "joo" for "you"—as well as an occasional "e" added to a word starting with "s" and her eccentric rearrangement of words within sentences that gave her speech an extra spice.

She followed a puff of smoke with "I welcome you to hell." Not a bad line, but she delivered it flatly without Luciferian conviction.

"Joo are here as a hostage. We are not in the business to take Anglos. We do this as a favor to a friend of the family. Who will say? We may want to do this new business. How do you say... an extension line?"

"Yes, very good. But in the corporate world we call it a line extension."

"What is the sense in that?"

I was sufficiently nervous to be eager to help. "If you have a product, say Tide detergent, you have the giant size and the small size and then the versions with and without bleach alternative and so on. We call that a line of products, and in a supermarket they would actually be lined up, so it makes some sense. Then, when you add..."

She waved off my lesson in consumer marketing with some annoyance. "Jes, jes—too much."

People just are not as curious about their products as they ought to be.

"Right. No problem."

"Here is what joo need to know. We are in the business to import. Here joo are in a warehouse for our imports. The merchandise is here till the cost is paid, including shipping and handling. Then it is delivered. Our product is very important to us, and we have much security to make sure we have no missing merchandise. This term I know from the one day I worked at WalMart: loss prevention. We have bars on the windows and the doors are locked from the outside and there are guards. My guards were all professional boxers, and if joo know the reputation for much fierceness of Mexican boxers, then you can imagine how they yearn to use this talent without a referee. Are you seeing my point?"

"That it would be pointless to attempt an escape."

"Pointless and painful."

Trying to make conversation I said, "It's interesting that you worked at WalMart. Where I work we make many products sold at WalMart."

"Fuck Walmart. Six hours on the job I decided that I would rather risk going to jail rather than be a prisoner by my choice."

"I see your point."

"Joo are difficult for us. My men do not all day wear estupid moustaches and glasses. Joo will be kept with our other merchandise, and if you see the merchandise, joo see the merchandise. Not a worry. But if one of my boxers comes into the room, it is joor duty to put on the special black glasses. Break this rule and joo will force me to decide whether to pull out joor eyeballs or just to kill you. Either one would be bad for my loss prevention. Joo comprehend?"

"I promise my full cooperation. There's just one tiny issue that maybe we should deal with upfront. May I explain?"

She blew smoke upward, over my head. Not certain what to make of this, I pressed ahead. "Here's the situation: I have no immediate family, no wife or children, my parents are deceased, and my employer won't pay for Girl Scout Cookies, much less hostage payments. You see the dilemma."

"Not for me, this dilemma. I am the warehouse. The money goes elsewhere. And now joo will go elsewhere, with the imports."

One of the henchmen leaned down to whisper to El Papagayo who nodded approval without enthusiasm. "Before joo join the others, we need pictures. Against that wall."

I was pushed toward an empty off-white wall, and one of the men produced a small digital camera. They messed with my hair and tie, apparently not wanting me to look as assured and buttoned-up as I do even under trying circumstances. Then, instead of a photo, there was an argument in Spanish that I couldn't follow, and it grew so heated that I thought two of the old boxers might go at it. I soon figured out that there was no newspaper for me to hold up to prove the date. Who gets a daily paper anymore? Not these modern consumers. Eventually they put me next to a television in the family room and tuned it to CNN, and we all had to stand around waiting for something specific to that day to appear. They settled for the Dow Jones report. The market fell 84.24. That was me, my Day One, down 84.24.

That would all have been fine with me, but an instant before snapping the picture, one of the men pulled a gun and fired into the wall near my head. I later was told that the little camera wasn't just for a photo but took a video and they decided I should look not just rumpled but terrified.

Yes, to looking terrified. They can put a gold star next to that one on their Team Goals for Today list. I still am finding drywall powder in my ear, something which definitely would not happen on the Concierge level of the Bellagio.

What You Find is Yourself

I WAS ASSIGNED TO THE BEDROOM that most people would call the master bedroom. I don't call it that because I work in HR, and we know that such a word conjures up unfortunate associations, especially in the southern region of the country. Thus have I learned to call it the *main bedroom*. (This invariably causes confusion, and I end up having to explain and there's no way to explain without mentioning the word I wasn't mentioning. So I remind them by not reminding them. Sigh. It's a burden being so sensitive.)

I was the only one who was not granted the freedom to move about the house, given that they did not want me to observe the goings-on of the place. The guards did not enter the main bedroom unannounced because that's where the women were given some measure of privacy. My presence caused resentments among some of the male merchandise and some made a point of shooting dark stares my way when they passed the open door.

Over the next week I learned that the headcount of the house changed daily, but the demographics hardly varied. About a third of the residents were women, plus a handful of children. The remainder were mostly young men in their twenties, although a few were middle-aged. My favorite fellow residents were a trio of older women, demographic oddballs like me, related to each other in some complicated way I didn't quite follow—Encarna, Anita, and Felipina. I came to think of them as my Tres

Madres. All three were short but sturdy and all three had long hair held back by a sliver clip at the crown. They spoke a bit of English and were eager to have me teach them new words as they pantomimed or pointed to objects in old magazines. During these lessons they laughed often and heartily, but were touchingly self-conscious of their lack of first-rate dental care, showing only a glimpse of teeth. One of them, Encarna, had one front tooth edged in gold. Having grown accustomed to African-American employees proudly showing gold teeth, I found her gold accent attractive but she wanted nothing to do with my compliments.

We ate twice a day, morning and late afternoon. Most everyone else ate standing around the family room, but I remained in the back. We were given eggs or meat with beans and rice and we always ate with tortillas. I don't just mean that each meal came with tortillas, but that we ate with tortillas as a utensil. No silverware, not even plastic substitutes; you scooped and mopped with tortillas. And what joy those tortillas visited upon my tedious days! Maybe it was the lard, maybe something in being handmade or in some authentic corn or flour, but for the rest of my days when some wine snob starts reminiscing about the wine of Bordeaux, I will counter with plumy praise of the perfect tortilla served to me as I sat on the dirty carpet of the generic house on Mystery Street.

Yes, it was a pleasure being fussed over by the Tres Madres, and yes I enjoyed the tortillas. I was grateful to pick up more Spanish. And there were some children to offer the occasional diversion, as well as many questions about life in the United States to answer. However, my predominant emotion was intense boredom, if that counts as an emotion. No work, no friends, no books, not even a window to stare out, the windows having been covered by white shades duct-taped in place to prevent even a peek at the outside world. There was no entertainment save for a television in the family room where I wasn't allowed, and where the programming was strictly Spanish-language. On one occasion someone in another bedroom started a folk song that the others took up, only to have the group immediately silenced by guards enforcing the rule that there be nothing to suggest to neighbors that there were thirty or forty of us inside this "single family" house.

My monotony brought back a memory of the time I visited a spa that offered sessions in an "isolation tank," floating in body temperature water inside a soundproof, lightproof shell. For half an hour I waited for a revelation that never arrived, and when the bearded guru of the tanks helped me step out of the little white submarine he asked what I'd seen. Apologetically I confessed that I'd mostly been bored.

He replied snippily, "What you find is yourself." Asshole.

Instead of being in a tank, I was in a body temperature room with the white noise of constant chatter in Spanish. There was one striking woman to covertly stare at, with lips that I could have written poems about if I had any paper to write on, but she was gone the day after I arrived. So, being human, or at least being a man, I found the next-best woman to fantasize about. She was shipped off that same afternoon. Next best. Next best.

You may have heard me say that boredom is your friend. I say it a lot at work. My thinking is that if you're bored, it's your brain issuing an invitation to try something new. In my first job I got so bored that I started looking at what was in the filing cabinets that lined the hall. I found old employment records, and that inspired me to find the records of the most successful sales people. I put together a hiring plan using the results. It didn't work, in that it didn't end up predicting future sales success, but it worked for my career. I was seen as a do-er and, more importantly as an HR guy who actually thought about sales. There's a lesson there: The next best thing to succeeding is failing. Fail up. It gets you noticed.

I Immediately Stopped Moping

FINALLY, AFTER A WEEK, I was called into the office. One of the Tres Madres gave me the news that she was to take me to the office. Two guards were there, wearing the moustaches and sunglasses, as was El Papagayo, although this time she did not wear the ball cap so I got to see the shiny red streak. (It was actually purplish-red. I'd call it by the accurate color of cerise, but that is the sort of fashion precision that gets you stereotyped—and you know what type is repeatedly attributed to my stereo.)

She gestured to a hard plastic chair meant for patio use. As it was my first chair in days, sitting in it felt so regally businesslike that I almost forgot to be nervous. After all, I knew that at some point my captors would get the response to their demands and I expected no compromise from Genghis... *unless*... maybe, just maybe, Carlota would intervene. Then I probably would have to marry her. You might toss that off lightly, saying to yourself, "Well, that's not a fate worse than death." But what is? During my week of boredom I started a mental list of such fates and became so morose as a result that one of the Tres Madres diagnosed melancholia and told the guards that I could only be cured by treatment with daily enemas. I immediately stopped moping. (Should I ever get back to my job, I'm going to try this suggestion on sulking employees.)

But back to the point. Unless Carlota convinced Genghis to cave, and I figured those odds at about one in a hundred, then sometime soon the kidnappers would have to send some up-the-ante threats that might include body parts. I'd been mentally steeling myself for a life without a pinkie finger or maybe an ear. I'd seen photos of human ears being grown in laboratories and my thoughts kept circling back to them—hostage porn.

Never had I been so ungrateful for being proved right as when El Papagayo said, "Man, joo ain't worth sheet. Nobody will pay for joo."

The blood left my pinkie fingers and my ears, leaving a crinkled aluminum feeling.

She continued. "But here's what I do not comprehend. The people who wanted joo taken, they were no surprised when joor company would not pay for joo. The man said to me, 'I thought so.' That was all—'I thought so.' Explain this to me. Who wants to kidnap a man without worth?"

While not pleased with the business about being without worth, I too was perplexed. If those behind my taking weren't stupid, what were they?

As is my way, I took a stab at an explanation. "There are people in my field who would go to great lengths to prevent me from winning the prize as HR Professional of the Year. Perhaps this is to get me out of the way for one of the other contenders. To name just one, there's a guy in Tucson who always struck me as being wholly without conscience." Even as I said it, it struck me as thin.

"This R-H award, it comes with large money?"

"HR. No, it's not a monetary award. But it is the highest award in the state and then there's regional and national. Some people would..." I started to say "kill for it," but didn't want that notion floating out into the cosmos, so I just looked down and mumbled, "...do almost anything."

While I was looking down she must have made some gesture, because there was coarse chuckling from the two guards.

Then, in rapid Spanish she gave instructions to the henchmen and they obediently shuffled out, closing the door behind them.

El Papagayo said solemnly, "Joo are going to be here some while. I have an offer to make. I want joo to work for me."

The feeling came back into my ears and pinkies, and I responded with gusto. Here was a chance to be something other than a nuisance and a drain on the reserves of beans and tortillas. "Yes, yes. That would be great. I am so bored. Let me think... for one, I'm a capable gardener. Or I could do some painting or I have a knack for wall papering and that would really brighten things up for the ladies in the main..."

"No, no. Do not be estupid. This is a rental."

"But I could do some yard work without raising suspicions about who is living here."

This struck her as hilarious. "Do joo really think that seeing Mexicans doing the jard work would cause suspicions? I could hide a thousand Mexicans by having them ride in old pick-up trucks with lawnmowers in the back. No, to see Anglos doing jard work, that might raise the suspicions."

She had a point. "Okay, not yard work. You tell me: How can I help?"

"I was hearing joo are a businessman. With a college degree?"

"Yes, an undergraduate degree in psychology and an MBA, a master's in business."

"This means joo know about running a business?"

"I work for a large corporation. I'm the head of Human Resources, so I help hire the talent, improve productivity, make sure we comply with all laws. I take care of the people who take care of the customers."

"This is running the business?"

"Yes, it is the most important part of the business, and I run it." This is something I would never have said in ordinary company, but here I figured my overstatement was unlikely to find its way back to Genghis Cone.

"Then joo could advise me. I am surrounded by men who would kill for me but who own no marketing snappy." She meant savvy, I presumed, but decided not to interrupt.

"I took one class in business at Mesa Community College, and for that my uncle puts me in charge of this operation. He thinks I should be the next El Chapo. You know this name?"

I nodded. (He heads one of the drug cartels in Mexico. For all I know he may have been captured by now, but he'd had an extraordinary run by criminal standards.)

"Jes, in Mexico he is a Donald Trump, only not a joke. He is what Donald Trump thinks Donald Trump is. He is an idol in Mexico. They write songs to him. And my uncle keeps telling me, Think like El Chapo, Think like El Chapo. But how do you think like someone you have never met? El Chapo has not written a book of what they call at Mesa Community a book of tips." She said it "teeps" and frowned when she did. "Tips? That cannot be right. That is for the waitress."

"No, *tips* is exactly right. It means valuable bits of advice you give, like giving money to a waitperson, but you're giving wisdom instead of money. And if you have a computer hooked up to the Internet, I could do some research, and you could quote him and maybe imitate some of his methods. That would impress your uncle."

"It's right here," she said, tapping on a laptop. "I will make joo a deal. Freedom of the house if joo promise to forget everything. If you tell the police about me or anyone here, then joo will be killed before you can testify. This is what joo call, how do you say it? Just business. Not personal."

There was that assertion again, whistling past my personal grave. "Yes, just business. And you have my word."

She stood and offered a hand, and we shook.

I grinned and assured her, "If it ever happens that the police question me, I will tell them that all I can remember is that you are of average height with dark hair and brown eyes."

"A bit taller than average, for my people. And joo can also tell them that I am unusually beautiful."

El Papagayo walked me into the family room and asked for the attention of the group. She announced that I had been named an honorary illegal and would now be free to use the entire house. At my request, she also explained that I was helping develop the business, and they should answer my questions. Only later did I realize that this meant that anyone in the room who ended up being questioned by immigration authorities could finger me as someone working for the cartel. I was an accessory to human smuggling. Imagine what that would do to my chances for grabbing off the HR Exec of the Year.

The Accessory

ALONE IN THE DARK that night I tried to work up some worry about legal exposure, but I called upon Putin and he wouldn't let me. He squatted next to where I lay on the carpet and congratulated me. I urged him to sit and stay, that I needed his advice.

"Sit on this filthy carpet in a four thousand euro suit. I have a tailor flown in from Saville Row to do the measurements. Feel the quality of this wool. No, stop. Don't touch. Your hands have been touching the carpet."

"Okay, fine, I'll stand with you. Come in the bathroom where we don't have to whisper."

Putin was impressed by the separate shower and pointed out "a nice sized tub, for a house built for commoners."

"What do you think," I asked him, "do I help them and become a criminal?"

"Criminal? You're still a prisoner. If you forget this is the situation, try pushing past that guard in the living room, and his fist will remind you."

"But in America, if you help a criminal, that makes you what we call an accessory to the crime, and that makes you a criminal too."

"Accessory? Like a tripod for a camera?"

"Yeah, but human."

"So you will get a criminal's nickname. You would be The Anglo Accessory." He threw out his hands and said "Boo!" This he found hilarious. "Ow, I am scared. Maybe too scared. Maybe it would be better if you were some other accessory, maybe The Pocket Square or The Cufflink."

"You make fun, but being an accessory would be a serious felony. So maybe I should only pretend to help them and give them fake advice."

"I have seen your Human Resources reports, and who would know the difference?" He was proud of this one and slapped my shoulder.

"I thought you were on my side," I responded sourly.

He gripped both my shoulders and gave me a comradely look. "Yes. I came to congratulate you. This is a better you. All those years of worrying about silly American labor laws and now, at last, you can take off your women's panties and be an outlaw. This is good! And this El Chapo will be a good study for you. Do you know what his name means?"

I told him that I didn't.

"The short one. Shorty. You and I both can look down. Two inches shorter."

Someone was tapping on the door, wanting to use the facilities. Three bathrooms in a four-bedroom house might be just fine, but not when you have thirty-some residents.

Putin playfully but painfully punched me in the chest and said, "You outlaw. Make the best of it."

Make the best of it. That's something else I often tell deflated employees, the ones who'd been given assignments they didn't want. "Every job is a chance to earn a better job," I advise them, along with, "You get a better job by being better than the job." That's when I realized that I'd already had plenty of experience at being an accessory. Or, as the young people would say, a tool.

Special Report

A MOST EXCELLENT DREAM was terminated by a pointed boot stabbing at my ribs. It was one of the boxers, and he grunted at me to follow him.

El Papagayo was in the office, face in the laptop computer on her desk. "This joo must see," she told me gleefully, pointing to the chair across the desk and turning the screen so that we could both watch. "Joo made the news. A special report, just about joo."

She hit Play, and there I was on screen doing an Edvard Munch scream, a frozen image that must have come from the video of them firing into the wall beside my head. Into the visual came the headline "Who Kidnapped Win-Win?" accompanied by echoing chords of electronic music.

The announcer was a smirky guy that I recognized but couldn't put a name to.

"Over the weekend we got news of a shocking crime. An American executive, forty-eight year-old Winslow Cheeseley, an executive with an American corporation, was kidnapped in broad daylight while a shocked neighbor looked on.

"The kidnapping for ransom of executives has become commonplace in Mexico and in South America, but is relatively unknown in the United States. Authorities fear the start of a new kind of sensational crime has come to our shores.

"In this special report, sponsored by M.I.C. Products—the value-priced products that might be even better than what you're using—we start with the account of Mrs. Virginia Misanni, a neighbor of the victim."

There was my neighbor, jaw set, holding one of her late husband's rifles, looking ready to singlehandedly chase crime back across the border.

"*Tell us what you saw.*"

"*This was no casual street violence. This was a well-planned attack. Real professional.*"

She described the nun in the wheelchair toppling over and my leaping out to give assistance. El Papagayo hit the Pause button and said, grinning, "This next part is my favorite. This I love."

Mrs. Misanni resumed. "*And then two men pulled up and one of them jumped out and helped the nun drag Mr. Cheeseley into the minibus.*"

"*What can you tell us about the two men?*"

"*I got a clear visual on the one that got out. He was a Chinaman.*"

"*A Chinaman? Not Korean or Japanese, but Chinese?*"

Mrs. Misanni didn't like being interrupted or doubted, and her response was frosty. "*I say Chinaman because he had a Fu Manchu mustache, but if your point is that he could have been from somewhere else, then fine.*"

This made El Papagayo hoot with delight, repeating her words, doing a perfect imitation of her voice.

"*And did you feel that this was an actual nun or just someone in costume, perhaps a man in disguise?*"

"*I'm sure it was a woman.*" (Another whoop from El Papagayo.) "*Also, I grew up in the Church and I know an actual nun when I see one.*"

The camera came back to the announcer who turned slowly to it, letting us admire his hair and note the condescending doubt on his features.

"*Now, here is the latest YouTube sensation, with three million views and counting.*"

There I was, against the wall in the room next to where

I currently sat, with CNN on the TV beside me, looking confused and jumpy. I'd forgotten that they had taken the time to make me look rumpled, having pulled my tie askew and given me spaghetti hair. Plus I'd picked up a grease stain from being hoisted into the van by hands that had just been on the asphalt. The overall effect was that I looked like a man who might just have been slapped awake in an alley after a night of sleeping in his own vomit.

But then there came the gunshot, and I jerked sideways in a *Lord of the Dance* quickstep as I squealed—and I mean full falsetto girly-squeal—"*Fudge! What the hay? Fudge! Oh, fudge meeee-eee!*"

REASON #36: Using faux expletives and curses that make you sound like an enraged third grader from the 1950s.

The announcer returned, making it clear he was reining in a laugh, "*With almost as many views, here's a sample of the musical version of Mr. Cheeseley's reaction.*" And there I was, set to music, screaming over and over. They'd added back-up vocals, turning me into a crazed Gladys Knight with my own set of jazzy Pips.

Bad. The situation was bad. Horrible. But not irreparable, I told myself. People are so accustomed to seeing outrageous behavior on YouTube that it passes through the standards of the conventional and into those of entertainment; it's the new vaudeville. I was just the clown of the day. Or so I, the Great Rationalizer, told myself and started to tell El P, but she shushed me and let the video play on.

The announcer: "*We meet now two people intimately involved in this story.*"

The screen filled with an in-studio shot of Genghis Cone in a gray suit and to his left sat Carlota in a stateswoman pants suit. But not the Carlota I knew so well. This one was wearing a new elegant cranberry satin, to go with a feathery new hairstyle and showing off the skills of a professional make-up artist who must have worked overtime.

Genghis was asked for details. *"I got a call. They used one of those voice synthesizers."*

El Papagayo paused the news report to boast in a mechanical voice, "That was me, pretending to be on a synthesizer." That's when I understood the nickname The Parrot might have had a different origin than I'd presumed.

"They told me that they had Cheeseley and they asked for an odd amount, nine hundred and ninety nine dollars. I thought it was a joke. Who kidnaps the HR Director? And that amount sounded like a play on what we call retail pricing."

"So what happened next?"

"I told them I was busy making M.I.C. Products even a better value and didn't have time to waste on practical jokes. That's when they told me about the video they'd made and that I should go online and watch it and they'd call back. I had an assistant watch, and she was convinced that it was real and so I informed Carlota to take a break from her work on our new line of M.I.C. Cosmetics. (Here the old salesman turned to look directly into the camera.) *She has created our new ALBB line, which stands for A Little Bit Better, meaning better than what you're overpaying for now."*

"And why did you believe it would be of special interest to your daughter?"

They'd been showing a close-up of Genghis but now went to a shot of the two of them as he looked at her dubiously and said with what struck me as phony cheerfulness, *"Because she's engaged to marry him."*

Fudge me! is just not strong enough to describe my

shock. Screwed. That's the word to describe how I felt. It was one thing to have a hint of faux romance for the sake of the Japanese or a fake engagement for the sake of the Arabs, but to go on national television and announce that we are to be wed?

Carlota did what the recently affianced do and girlishly extended her left hand, and the studio lights exploded off the ring.

"And how are you holding up, Carlota?"

"My father is my role model, and he always taught us to turn our pain into productivity. So I don't let myself think about poor Winslow, I just keep working on the new ALBB Cosmetics. They really are better."

I now understood why they'd invested in a miracle worker of a make-up artist to do her up, and it also dawned on me that Genghis had immediately seen the PR possibilities of the situation, the millions in free advertising. My being taken was a gift from the gods of marketing.

"Back to the hostage situation. Did you urge your father to pay the ransom and get your fiancé back? After all, it was a tiny amount by corporate standards."

"Yes, I did. But Daddy reminded me that Win wouldn't want us to give in to criminals. My Win would want us to stay strong. As it happens when you run a successful company, there are people who try to take advantage and do slimy things like threatening us with frivolous lawsuits. Whenever that happened Win was the first one to take a hard line and say that we should never set a precedent by taking the easy way out and buying a short-term solution."

Here I had to admire the work of our PR consultants, who must have spent sleepless nights coming up with a way to make it my own principled fault if I got killed.

The announcer thanked the Cones and then pivoted to face a new guest, a former police detective who was now labeled a Special Correspondent, and asked his opinion on my chances of survival.

"Realistically, one option for the kidnappers is to execute him and put his body in a vat of lye, and he is simply never heard from again. However, if this is the start of a new crime trend, they could execute him on video as an example for the employers or families of future victims. That way taking him would still serve a grim purpose, and their efforts wouldn't have been for naught."

El Papagayo turned to me and said, "I like this guy. He makes the good point." Then she winked.

"We'll take a break and when we come back we will continue our analysis and ask the hottest question since, Who killed JR?—Who kidnapped Win-Win?"

With that, they played a bit more of the music video of me shrieking about fudge.

With sad eyes El Papagayo said, "I am afraid joo did not come to be a Mr. James Bond. More like Pussy Galore seeing a spider. If I had gotten to know joo before the video, I would have given you another shake."

"Take."

"Yes, take. Now we see the rest. It's very funny and not because of joo. This policeman is a balloon."

I suppose she meant buffoon, but suddenly weary, I didn't correct her and she eagerly fast-forwarded to the detective responding to questions from the announcer.

"What are you hearing from your sources—do they feel they are close to any breakthroughs?"

"My sources tell me that they are perplexed by this entire situation. Typically in an executive kidnapping the ransom demand is in the millions. This demand, less than a thousand dollars, doesn't make sense."

"I've heard people referring to Cheeseley as The Discount Hostage."

"One theory is that the kidnappers just didn't understand American business and grabbed a Human Resources guy. Then, realizing their mistake, went in with a low-ball demand just hoping to make a quick transaction. But the prevailing theory is that these are not professional kidnappers. After all, with a nun involved, we think there might be some other motive. The company has a reputation for being very stingy with its workers and they have had repeated layoffs. There is the possibility that this is an attempt at revenge. This could be the start of worker activism."

"Any other theories the authorities are investigating?"

"There's always the chance in a situation like this that it's a stunt. We've heard that Mr. Cheeseley is obsessed with winning a professional award, and that this might be somehow connected. But then you look at that video and no. Just no. That's no way to enhance your reputation in any field. That was real terror."

"And here was a man who was just engaged. He's in his late forties and never married, so it was a big step for him." There was something in the way he said it that let the audience wonder what the real question was.

"There are rumors about his engagement not fitting his, uh, sexual orientation, so that's another avenue one could pursue."

"You're saying that he's gay, and this is all to get out of marrying Ms. Cone?"

"I'm not saying that, no. But others are pointing out the inconsistencies, that he is a member of a LGBT Advisory Committee for a Senator, and that fudge is a loaded word in that community. So there are suspicions."

"Bizarre. We'll all be following this story."

A World Where No One Cared About YouTube

AS YOU UNDOUBTEDLY saw on television or online, I was briefly a big story, even rating a day-by-day counter: Who Kidnapped Win-Win? Day Five...Day Six... on and on. Carlota was everywhere, sporting a new wardrobe and image, and worrying aloud about my safety only briefly before talking about how her cosmetics line was "keeping her sane and giving her hope." She even did a full hour on one of the shopping networks, where the fate of one Win-Win Cheeseley was dispensed with in the first fifteen seconds so as to get on to the more demanding issue of reducing pore size.

Had I been in my normal life, all this nonsense being said about me would have been an overwhelming burden, and I would have had to pull out my old Tony Robbins CDs to keep up my spirits. However, the whole point was that I was not in my old life. I was living in a world where no one cared about YouTube. Imagine that.

More importantly, I had my work to keep me busy. I studied this El Chapo in search of business wisdom that would allow El Papagayo to "Think like El Chapo." I found one particularly helpful piece in the *New York Times* where the writer took a serious look at El Chapo the executive. After all, the conservative estimates of his organization put it at three billion in revenues, roughly the size of Netflix or Facebook. However, those two companies have it easy by comparison, not having to work around law enforcement or deal with homicidal competitors.

What impressed me most about the guy's business was its diversity, bringing in drugs via dozens of routes and schemes. He has a fleet of small submarines, and should one of them be intercepted, the crew pops out in life jackets and lets the sub fill with water and sink, along with the evidence. And when a new fence was put across one popular land route into the U.S., he acquired a catapult able to toss one-hundred pound bales of marijuana over it.

These were the tactics being written about; thus, they were merely the ones gone bad. Imagine how many others there are, and they must be even better, because they have yet to be detected. Put another way, this endlessly creative and demanding El Chapo is the Steve Jobs of the drug business.

I explained as much to El Papagayo and suggested that the two of us go to an Apple Store for inspiration. She pointed out that a recent poll had found that more people could identify my face than any businessperson with the exception of Donald Trump or the late Steve Jobs; thus, I wasn't going anywhere. I offered to wear the nun disguise, but she reminded me that nuns everywhere were being given the stink eye of suspicion, given the public belief that one had snatched me.

We had many long conversations about business philosophy, and I was able to get my young "client" to stop thinking about the business as being about her and start thinking about it as being about her customers. It took some persuading, but as someone who was accustomed to dealing with Genghis Cone, I made quick work of convincing her that the language used around the "warehouse" did matter and persuaded her to stop referring to "the imports" and "the merchandise" and instead evaluate "the customer experience" of "our guests."

What she'd never considered—what do they teach in these community college business classes?—was repeat business. A large percentage of undocumented aliens are deported, and most of those merely save up their money and try again. Moreover, the ones who succeeded in taking up residence became a source of information to those still below the border.

I'd about convinced her to improve the customer experience when she suddenly resisted and barked out, "No, you have it wrong. Making nice to the merchandise would not be joor win-win. It would be win-lose, and the loser is your friend El Papagayo. We want them to beg their families to pay up and get them out. We can't be nice or we never get paid."

This had me stumped, but then as is so often the case when the Cheeseley brain starts whirring, a solution flew out from deep within: "Every problem carries the seeds of its solution. In this case, all you do is charge by the day. A flat rate plus a daily rate. So the longer they stay, the more you make."

That logic won her over and eventually changed her approach from being a warehouse to being a kind of hotel.

Of all our further conversations there was one moment that stands out because it produced our informal mission statement. (I just noticed that I said "our." That's the kind of team player I am. Put on the handcuffs, but darn it, that's just the way we Cheeseleys are built.)

"Sometimes it helps," I offered, "to imagine just one person—someone you know well, like a friend or relative—and design the business just for that one person."

"That would not be my father for he is dead and an asshole before that. And not my mother because she would complain no matter what I did. My sisters? One is too nervous and one too young. My small brother? Jes.

He is the one. We will make an experience of which my brother would boast."

Within days we had created a little crowded resort. No Bellagio, but she acquired aluminum cots such as the ones you see in disaster relief centers. And suddenly we had wonderful meals. These didn't even cost much because our customers were people used to eating economically and all she did was invite them to volunteer to make whatever they made best. She also found a sympathetic priest to hold mass twice a week. And we had English lessons, including language immersion where she allowed Spanish only an hour a day. (This last initiative transformed me from village idiot to professor.)

What didn't fit in with the new customer-oriented approach were the old guards. In corporate life we often refer to company traditionalists as the Old Guard, but here I had to literally deal with the old guards, the used-up boxers who were used to bullying the "merchandise" and not eager to become the concierge desk for the new resort atmosphere. This forced me to call upon my HR magic.

I convinced El Papagayo to set up a profit-sharing plan, although one key component, the "open books" policy, had to be left out for the compelling reason that there were no books.

I began holding HR seminars with the guards, who were now called Guest Relations Specialists. I had daily role-playing sessions, using as a translator the one GRS who had excellent English. I had a lot of work to do. Here's an example of the starting point from which I had to work.

"We have a rule that we can't allow our guests to go outside. So here's the situation: Pretend I'm a guest, and I come to you and say, 'I'm getting claustrophobic. I have to go out into the yard. Just for a minute. Please.' So what do you say?"

The GRS grabbed me by the shoulders and roughly turned me around while scoffing, "*Pendejo*," and shoving me back into the family room.

(For your edification, *pendejo* is an interesting insult because it literally translates to "pubic hair." I wouldn't have thought of that one.)

These ex-boxers often turned bashful when it came to employing verbal skills, but then again, one of the things you learn working in HR is that just about everyone detests role-play. (When you encounter someone who enjoys it, never pick that person to participate because you will have yourself a know-it-all and a ham who will steal the attention and ruin the effect.)

I began to construct an Employee Handbook, which I believe to be the first of its kind, meaning the first one for members of a criminal organization. We had a dress code and a conduct code and vacation policies and all the rest, including rules about harassment. It was the new sexual harassment policy that set off a particularly troubling round of role-playing. For one thing, someone had to play the part of a female customer, and that ended up being me, which the boxers found hysterical. They got endlessly playful when it came time to simulate the new customer intake, with its police-style pat-down for weapons. My pecs are still sore, not to mention my glutes.

I decided to train one of the Tres Madres to take over that particular task... patting down the female guests, I mean, not being subjected to the role play. Losing that favorite piece of their jobs to Encarna caused a near revolt among the ex-boxers, and eventually El Papagayo herself had to intervene in the spiraling dispute. I admired her creative compromise, which was to bring in a hooker to be patted-down in the back room. The young woman must have done some patting of her own, because it became a hugely popular job perk, even more popular than pizza day.

You Might Wonder
If I Felt Any Guilt

THERE'S ALWAYS A RELEASE of energy when an organization is being transformed, as if two chemicals had been poured together and begun to bubble. It amazed me how much we could accomplish in so short a time, but then again I didn't have anything else to do, and with El P as our benevolent dictator, decision-making was streamlined, usually with a simple, "Do it." By the time of "Who Kidnapped Win-Win? Day 64," we had made enormous strides in creating a first-rate organization. Yes, 64 days! Morale had soared, and so had customer satisfaction, and El Papagayo's uncle had declared her a genius and started talking about a promotion that would put her in charge of operations for the entire state.

I made use of the new camaraderie to ask El P if I could have a favor. I wanted to make a phone call and let people know that I was doing okay. Not that I was so eager to leave; the truth is, I was enjoying myself. It was a vacation.

(You might wonder if I felt any guilt about being part of a criminal activity. I kept asking myself the same thing, and the result was that I felt guilty only about not feeling guilty. I could rationalize this by saying that I was not bringing anyone into the country illegally, not adding to the problem, merely making the immigrants who were here a little safer and much more comfortable. And I wasn't profiting from it, either. But here's the most important piece: I liked the people. I liked my new colleagues and our customers, too. In my heart I wanted them to succeed in finding better lives. I wanted to help them. My new goal was to figure out how to guide El P into the business of legal immigration.)

Even though I was content to stay a while longer, I worried about the stress of my prolonged absence on my friends and colleagues back in the normal world, the one where windows let in light. I told El P that I wanted to find a way to make contact with those in my old life and that their knowing I was safe would be of benefit to her because it would help the media lose interest and that might mean the police would lose interest too.

El Papagayo's response surprised me. "I want to help joo to be happy here, Win-Win. I want joo to stay with me. I will make joo a good offer to work here with me. Joo can be my Operations Chief." This was the first unsolicited job offer I'd had in two decades, and it touched me, as did hearing what El P said next, with concern on her face: "Is this appropriate, to use the word 'chief,' or is that an insult to Native Americans?" Here was an executive who wanted to do the right thing and wanted to prove it to me. She had a point, too. Should we eliminate the word?

"You are a good friend and a good leader and I thank you," I replied formally to convey my appreciation and respect. "I am starting to think that we could find a way to make this business legal, and if so, I would be honored to be in charge of Operations. But till then, I would like to tell the people in my other life not to worry."

"We could make another video. Joo could not squeal this time."

"I'd rather just make a phone call. Or I could write a letter and have one of your men drop it in a mail box."

"For joo, a phone call. But we cannot call from here. We

use disposable cell phones and from places where else."

"Elsewhere. And I'd enjoy getting outside."

She looked pained. "But please do not try to run, because I do not want to have to hurt joo, and joo must stay and finish the Handbook and the new Values Statement and all the other."

"I will sit between two GRSs, handcuffed to the seat. And you have my promise, my word that I shall return." The last part was over-the-top, I know, but El P had an exaggerated sense of honor, one of her many attractive character traits.

They didn't have me wear handcuffs, but I was given a ball cap, sunglasses and a mustache, and two men accompanied me. Knowing this drive was coming, I'd thought through whom to call. Because I don't have immediate family and wanting someone local, I finally settled on Reggie. He'd be the one I could trust to help with some personal details like getting mail and transferring money to pay bills, and he would be the best to carry my message to Genghis, Carlota, and the police.

He answered his cell, as he almost always did, and he seemed pleased to hear from me, but not surprised.

"Where are you? I'm on my way."

I explained that it wasn't that kind of call and that I was still a hostage. Being preeminently practical, he began inviting me to offer clues as to my whereabouts by pretending to make touristy chat with questions like, "How's the weather where you are?" and "Did you see the smoke from the big fire by South Mountain last night?"

"Don't worry about me or trying to find me. I'm fine. Really. They are going to release me before long. They're having me do some work for them. It's a long story, and I'll tell it to you when I see you." I then asked for some favors and had a list to read to him. I explained where I'd hidden a key to my condo and asked him to get the mail and other domestic details. When I got to the list of tasks for those at the office, he stopped me.

"That's complicated," he said, and I felt the truth wrestling against friendship, deciding how much to say. Eventually he explained. "There's a new woman who's calling herself the new HR Director. But Kyle [FullOfHimself] has been spending a lot of time trying to undermine her and he told me, said it was a secret, that she's just a trial employee and not on the payroll and that he, Kyle, is planning to replace you and wants my help. He had the balls to tell me that it's what you would want. He actually put out a report and said that the odds of you being alive were now at seventeen percent and falling."

Well, well… the King is dead; long live the King. And here I'd been worried that the stress of worrying about me was causing a run on Rolaids.

Dropping his voice, Reggie added, "If you can get word to me, I'll get a team and extract you and we can put an end to this crap."

"Let me think about how to handle that."

"I also have here a memo from Mr. Cone. He instructs us that anyone who hears from you is to insist that you call him immediately. He gave us a special number, a cell phone straight to him."

After hanging up with Reggie, I got permission to make a second call, but only after the guard had checked with El P and we'd driven a while and then, after dialing the number Genghis had provided, he took the phone and tossed it into the back of a gravel truck and turned in a different direction. This struck me as harsh, toying with me, but then he produced a second phone, dialed the number again and told me I had two minutes.

Genghis was delighted to get my call, a first. He said, "I want you to know that what's happened with you has changed me and how I see the world. I'm a different person."

I found myself slipping right back into my old toady persona, coming across with this whopper: "There was nothing wrong with the old you."

"No, I've seen the light. I've changed."

"Me too. I've realized how precious our lives are and how quickly things can change. It's humanizing."

He chuckled. "I'm not sure what rainbow dust you've been snorting, but I'm talking about my discovery about branding. This new cosmetic line is a huge hit. A huge premium-priced hit. And I mean *premium*. For all these years we've been the value brand and now, we're *the* brand. Nordstrom's called me and begged for an exclusive. Begged."

With my old reflexes still in perfect shape, I manufactured instant faux enthusiasm. "That's great. Just great."

"I need to talk to your captors. The first number they gave me no longer works. I need to talk to them about you, right away. I want to reopen the negotiations."

"That's good to hear, particularly coming right after I heard a rumor that you'd replaced me."

"Win, Win, Win. Would I do that?"

The correct answer was "In a heartbeat," but I didn't say that or anything else because I got the signal that my time was up and could only say, "I have to go" and the GRS returned to his old role as grouchy guard and snatched away the phone. At the next red light he stepped out of the car and stuck it in the bumper of a UPS truck idling at the curb.

Imagine My Surprise

TWO DAYS LATER there was a meeting to decide my fate. Genghis had reopened negotiations with El Papagayo's uncle, and the two agreed to send representatives to work out the conditions of an exchange. El P decided to go herself, though I tried earnestly to dissuade her, worried about a police trap. However, she trusted the complicated scheme she'd worked out with the ex-boxers to insure that the meeting would be secure.

I distracted myself from worrying about her and my fate by conducting a seminar with our customers that I was calling Think Like an American. We were practicing the use of U.S. currency when a GRS told me that El Papagayo had returned and wanted me in her office.

I have a rule that I never let myself be interrupted when I'm leading a seminar, refusing to break my magic training spell, but my curiosity pulled me away and I slipped into the office. El P was at her desk, and imagine my surprise when the person sitting across from her turned to me and... "Carlota?"

She jumped up and gave me an intense hug and held it far too long, turning me as she hugged me, and I saw that she was posing us as one of the boxers was taking cellphone photos. She let go but then reached up and held my face in her hands and waited like a tennis champion staring at the trophy while letting the photographers get the perfect shot. She leaned in and whispered, "Don't get a boner yet." Later I would see my wild-eyed blushing response in a photo that was all over the news, undoubtedly chosen by Mundane's PR department for release because Carlota's make-up looked perfect.

"Am I leaving with you?" I asked, not at all certain of which response I was hoping for.

With a pout you might give a child who was not going to the Disney movie after all, she said, "Oh, my poor baby. No. Not yet. But there's a special treat for you in the deal I negotiated."

She turned to El Papagayo and said, "Could we have a minute alone?"

With a smirk, a shrug, and an exchange of glances with the boxer, she stood and gestured for the boxer to leave with her.

When we were alone, I offered my cold assessment: "So your father isn't paying the ransom, after all."

"Yes he is. I brought the down payment with me. You're not the Discount Hostage after all. You're now a premium brand, just like my cosmetics."

She was still standing too close. "And even though you have to stay a while, I negotiated a treat for you." She moved in and gave me kitten licks about the mouth. "Conjugal visits," she purred.

I tried to think of a kindly way to decline the invitation but I had been a month without female companionship and my wiener was putting itself on the hot roller, ready for the tongs of eros, any eros. "Just as soon as I get back from L.A. where we're shooting the next installments for the shopping networks." My hot roller stopped cold.

"But what about my work? My department?"

"Don't worry."

Prepared to be firm with her, I pulled her hands away from my face. Just then a cellphone on the desk began shouting "Goallllll, Goalllll," a crazed soccer announcer as a ringtone, and El P briskly reentered to retrieve it, giving a world-weary smile to the loving couple.

Carlota, instead of jumping back in embarrassment like any normal person, turned and said, "Is there a bedroom we could use?"

"I'm afraid that the bedrooming must wait. We must get joo back to your meeting point."

El P signaled for the boxers to return, and Carlota kissed me goodbye, putting a lot of tongue into it, and my rat of a pecker lurched about trying to jump ship and go with her.

I reached down to adjust my pants and one of the boxers caught me doing it. What is the protocol? What's the etiquette? In the current situation, all I could do was to quickly fold into a chair while saying idiotically about Carlota, "We work together." It must have occurred to the guard nearest me that I also worked with him, because he instinctively stepped in a boxer's stance.

Eager to change the subject I asked El Papagayo to explain the plan that she'd negotiated with Genghis via Carlota. She stared at me, deciding how much to tell me, then said, "This boss is not a good man. Joo are to be his family, to marry his daughter, and yet he sells joo like a rental car, by the week."

"It's a long story, but I'm not really engaged to Carlota." Trying for nonchalance, I added with a manly chuckle, "She isn't even my type."

Given that I was still hunched over a hard-on, this assertion went over about as well as the man holding a bloody axe while standing over a dead body insisting, "This isn't what it seems."

"Joo got her pregnant and are not going to marry her?"

"No! She isn't pregnant. I think she has a thyroid problem."

"A woman knows when another woman is pregnant. She tells joo she is not?"

"She's been that way a lot longer than nine months. Really."

"It is not my truth to untell. But joo should not be a part of that family. They told me they did not want joo back."

"That was just Carlota being a tough negotiator. She didn't mean that. And there's the proof." I pointed at the large envelope she held, gaping open with the cash inside. "She told me that they'd come through with a down payment and more would follow."

"They paid me to keep joo. They want to keep going on television to talk about how much they want joo back. It sells much product."

"I suppose it's worth millions of free publicity. How much are they paying you?"

"They offered a hundred dollars a week. I told them that putting a dog in the Pet Hotel at PetSmart cost more than that."

This surprised me. "I didn't know you had a dog."

"I don't have a dog. I have a television."

"Right."

"So I pretended to call and tell them to drop joo at the nearest Walmart, and she panicked and said five thousand a week. They really do not want joo back."

"No other conditions?"

"Conjugal visits, but that cannot be good for the baby."

"I'm happy to take those off the table. But that's it? No timetable? No plan?"

"She wants us to send a finger to them."

"What? My finger?"

"No, not jour finger. She told us to use one of the people we were killing anyway. That by the time the police told them it wasn't jours that it would—how she say?—add another bicycle on the news? Does this make sense?"

"Add another news cycle. She means that it'll be something more for them to report on television."

"Yes, news cycle. So joo are not to worry, she loves joo enough to want joo to have all ten fingers to hold on her. Just not enough to have joo and joor fingers back together with her."

This did not disappoint me like it should have. In fact, I was secretly pleased that I'd be able to work on the new employee suggestion program. "I guess you'll have me around a while."

She didn't return my smile. "It isn't up to me. I did not choose to take joo. I did it for my uncle, who did it for someone else. That person will decide and will get the money. All I get is the thanks of my uncle." She'd been avoiding my eyes and seemed annoyed, even angry. But then she softened and turned to face me. "But I am glad joo will be here to consult for me. Joo are a wise man, worthy of the name Win-Win."

Although I shouldn't have, I suppose, I felt a bubbling gratitude. I've gotten so little appreciation over the last years that even a compliment from a junior criminal felt like the sun coming out. "That's kind of you to say."

"No problem. I wish I could be of help to joo."

"It would be good if you could find out who had me kidnapped. It troubles the mind, not knowing who your enemies are."

With a grimace of sympathy she said, "I do not have a name and I have not met this person. I was to meet with him, but the plan was changed. I will see if I can learn a name, but that is not likely." She brightened. "One moment. I do know one thing. He has a tattoo. That was how he was to prove to me who he was, to show it to me when we met. It's on his hip. A bee. Buzz, buzz. Odd, no?"

Odd, yes. But, but, but… Was it possible? I knew one person who had a bee tattoo: FullOfHimself! I'd never seen the thing, but he said it was on his lower back, which could be described as a hip. What are the odds?

"Did they give you any details about the man or the tattoo?" I squeeked.

"They told me he was a young white guy, and the bee in the tattoo was following some trail to somewhere, I can guess it was into his pants to his estupid…"

She interrupted herself to snicker at my reaction. "Joo look like a goldfish whose bowl has broken."

Why would he do such a thing? It made no sense, unless he knew that I was planning to get rid of him. I hadn't said anything to him or to anyone else. I had a secret file on his ineptitude. Could he have found out? What file is truly confidential these days?

"I think I know who it is, but it makes no sense." I explained my suspicions and my reasoning.

"Joo are above him. He wants joor job. Esimple."

"No, he isn't anywhere near being qualified. He couldn't have thought that."

"My uncle always complained that every soldier believes he knows more than the general. Now that I work for my uncle, I know what he means—I could do his job better than he does it."

"I wish I had some proof. I can't very well ask you to turn him over to the police."

"My uncle would have me killed if I went to the police. At least that's what I would do if I took over from my uncle." An eagerness in her eyes as she said this last bit showed that she was cozying up to the idea of replacing Old Unc.

"I need evidence. There must be a way."

Trying on the role of wise uncle, she said, "Joo have a truth. A useful truth. Too useful to waste on police."

A Cooler in the Shape
of a Giant Coke Can

I T TOOK TWO DAYS TO ARRANGE, but I was able to have another phone call with Reggie. Again I was taken out for a drive and given a disposable cellphone.

Once I'd explained about the tattoo and my conclusions, Reggie suggested that the next step would be to tie the bastard to the original threat, the cartridge on the desk, and assured me that he would get fingerprints from FullOfHimself that very afternoon and could get a preliminary result within a day or two.

That business out of the way, he told me he was worried for my job. "That new woman in HR, Linda something, has settled into your office. At first she was saying she was Acting Director, but lately the Acting is getting left off. She's been meeting every day with a different department. She calls them Lunches with Linda."

"Corny. I bet she's generating more resentments than allies."

He added gravelly, "She's been bringing pizza."

"Ha. Laughable. You think a couple of pizzas are going to make people forget all my years at the company?"

He paused longer than you'd want a friend to pause. "Well, it *is* good pizza, from Rosati's, which people keep comparing to the frozen stuff you used to offer up. And then they remember that even the frozen ones got eliminated and after that you started brown-bag lunches where people had to bring their own. I don't know if they said this to your face, but they were known as the lunchless-lunch. So the pizza comes across big."

"You think I wanted to chintz out on the pizza? Nooo. I had budget cutbacks just like everyone else. But even then, I provided sodas. That was a triumph of budget stretching."

"Hey, I'm on your side here, Win. And some people like RC Cola and the Kroger store brand, but mostly not-so-much, so when she wheeled in a cooler in the shape of a giant Coke can, people... well, let's just say that people are shallow."

That hurt. A party cooler of genuine Coke product? This was serious. "Yes, they are. I just wonder who approved the budget for some silly cooler." I called it silly, but I could picture the sturdy red plastic and the round, clear plastic lid on a hinge and the carbonated joy I would have felt wheeling one into an HR seminar. That's the sort of thing they do at Apple or Google, not at Mundane Industries. At least not before they discovered the luxury of being a premium product, driven by my captivity.

Reggie interrupted my dispirited thoughts with even darker news. What does it take to make your problems seem small? A much larger problem. "I do have something else to report. Carlota came to see me today, and I helped her set up another meeting. She told me that you were going to get paid back for all your trouble and she would personally do the paying."

That could only mean one thing: the conjugal visits. No, no, no.

But Reggie must not have known about the conjugals because he kept talking, being upbeat and congratulatory. "She didn't explain that, but I took it to mean that you're getting some sort of cash settlement for hanging in there while they work the PR. You deserve it."

I decided there was no reason to keep any secrets from this good man. "I'm afraid it isn't money she's referring to. She's planning to give herself to me. She negotiated conjugal visits."

There was another long pause, and I knew that all his military training was being brought to bear, keeping him from blurting out sympathetic profanities and objections. Instead, I realized, he was stifling his laughter. "That photo of the three of you at the charity ball has been going around the office, and here I was, insisting that it was a Photoshop fake."

I could only hope he didn't mean the embarrassing one. "The three of us?" I asked, hopefully.

"Yeah. You, Carlota and the salami in the slacks. I guess you really do have the hots for her. I wouldn't have guessed it, but you live as long as I have, you stop guessing."

So the photo had gone public, as everything does in this time of over-exposure. "That's going around? How did that get out? That's a very misleading salami, er, photo. That was meant for someone else. I agreed to play at being a couple, and now she's taken it into her head that we really are."

I wanted his advice, but my time was up—I'd already been given two impatient warnings—and the phone was jerked away and tossed into the back of a construction truck waiting at the next light.

Go Ahead and Shoot

T HAT NIGHT I HAD A VIVID SEX DREAM starring Carlota. I blush at the thought and will not elaborate. No, not even a hint. I bring it up only because I found myself falling back into a waking version of that dream, repeatedly. This makes no sense. I've never been certain that I had a *type*, but I feel certain that no one was attracted to the type to which Carlota belonged. I've never been attracted to hairy or bossy or manly women; no, not a bit, just the opposite. But put those fully undesirable traits together and what do you have? Me, fantasizing about a rendezvous.

Perhaps it is being in captivity that makes you grasp at any straw. Perhaps there's some weird inversion of the sexy-beast fantasy going on in my head. Perhaps it's the same stupid contrariness that makes people put an apple on their head and say, Go ahead and shoot it.

Thank goodness I have my work to make me forget about Carlota. I got us some poster board and tape, and all of us—the GRSs and the guests—have been putting up motivational sayings and it's really quite uplifting. We really are in the business of hope. It's uplifting to be around people who are boldly undertaking new lives, risking savings and their safety for something better. Contrast this to my coworkers at M.I.C., who feel their futures were being sucked out of them, taking life one day at a time as if in a twelve-step program to overcome an addiction to believing.

A New and Gruesome Twist

ONE MORNING BROUGHT A SURPRISE. I was called into El Papagayo's office—nothing unusual about that, as I spent hours with her practically every day—but she was furious, something I hadn't seen before.

She showed me a video of a newscast. It was now Day 92 in my saga, a good eighty-nine days past the freshness date on a news story, and I now rated only scant mention. But this time I was again Breaking News.

"There's a new and gruesome twist in the story of the kidnapping of Phoenix executive Winslow Cheeseley. Today his employers received a package containing a finger. In a heartwrenching turn of events, the package was opened by Carlota Cone, the woman engaged to be married to Mr. Cheeseley."

There was Carlota with perfect hair and make-up, wearing the frowny look you'd give a child who'd gotten a nasty paper cut, explaining that the kidnappers had sent her not just a finger but a special message; it appeared to be the ring finger of the left hand.

I know this is stupid, but I confess it: I found myself glancing down to make sure all my fingers were still there.

The announcer came back on. *"So they've given you the... Well, they sent this message. Is there a message you want to give them? They probably are watching; after all, we are the trusted source for the news you need."*

"I do want to say that I don't believe them. This does not look like it belongs to the man I'm going to marry. I think it may be some sick prank or something to distract me from my

search for Winslow."

"That would create a new mystery. You can bet we'll be following it."

"Could I just take a minute to thank everyone who has offered support, especially those who have bought my new line of M.I.C. cosmetics. You don't know how much it helps get me through all this. Thank you."

While I saw much to admire in how Carlota had played the interview, El Papagayo was fuming, and in blazing Spanish so I had no idea what was troubling her. After a while she returned to English and explained that the finger did not come from her or her uncle and that it would reenergize the police investigation and lead to more charges if the authorities should make arrests.

Was Carlota in on the finger? Genghis? It didn't seem possible, but then who was I to question any of life's possibilities or impossibilities while spending my days doing excellent work for a criminal enterprise and about to be married to a woman who simultaneously gave me nausea and a hard-on.

You Have Two Hours

THE DAY CAME FOR MY "CONJUGAL VISIT," and my heart and head were in a muddle, unlike the lower regions which thought it was Mardi Gras and had the mojitos ready.

The plan was simple. I was to be driven to a hotel room by one of the boxers. A guard, one of the uncle's men, would be there waiting outside while I was in the room, then afterwards the boxer would return to pick me up and escort me back to the house. Because Genghis and Carlota didn't want me returned, it was in no one's interest to involve the police or let me escape—except mine, and even I wasn't sure about that.

For some reason, everyone in the house, the thirty-some current guests, and all the GRSs, knew of the plan and there was much whooping and hip thrusting prior to my departure.

As I was being driven to the hotel, I thought to ask if there was a time specified or if I was just to emerge whenever it suited me, or more likely, Carlota.

"You have two hours."

Two hours? I'd been so preoccupied trying to rationalize being physically attracted to Carlota that I hadn't given any thought to the actual time.

Two hours? I'd had occasions to be in a sexual hurry—the rendezvous over the lunch hour or the quickie before a social function or on the not unpleasant occasions of getting it over before one of us fell asleep. On the other side of the bed, there were all those times when we'd had all night. But two hours? That was something else. The best use of the time seemed to me to get right to it, then chat a while, recharging the battery, then go again. But with Carlota I wouldn't be the one making decisions. Would she expect a long, slow build? Or would she crave a marathon?

The driver pulled up to a motel, a decent one, although we entered off a side street so I didn't see the name. Whoever had picked the place had chosen wisely. There were half a dozen rooms in the back corner, facing some landscaping and then a massive concrete wall that, based on the hum of engines and tires, ran along a freeway. It was unlikely anyone would see us arrive or leave. Also there was a courtyard with patio furniture, and there sat a guard, not one of my GRSs but someone the uncle had sent to make sure I didn't run. Having feared that the guard might be in the room with us, this was a relief. My boxer-driver gave a sniggered farewell, clapping me on the back and telling me to be strong. "Two hours," he repeated. "I'll be back in plenty of time. Don't come out till you see me parked here."

The uncle's guard was also in on the joke that was my new love life and raised his giant Starbucks cup in salute and made kissing noises.

Maybe it was having spent a month with virtually no privacy and with no sex partner, or maybe it was confronting my own sexual dark side, but I found myself twitching in anticipation of the embracing the opposite of what had always attracted me. I was nervous as a virgin schoolboy. The door was cracked open, and it was dark inside, which described my sense of myself at that moment.

I knocked gently as I entered, trying to make it a playful and romantically musical rhythm, which is something even a schoolboy would have to acknowledge was ridiculous, but there I was.

And there Carlota was, under the sheets, cooing. I closed the door, and finding that the only light was from around the edges of the curtains, I let my eyes adjust. I went to the side of the bed and sat. In the dim light I could see only her hair and eyes. "Finally, we are alone together," she said in a hoarse whisper.

"Finally," I repeated. Now, when the time had come, my wiener was strangely passive. Not a twitch.

"Was the guard drinking the Starbucks?" she asked, and I wondered if she was nervous too, asking such an irrelevant question.

"Yes. He seemed content out there." As I spoke, I let my hand slide up her arm, and then over her shoulder and inside the sheets, journeying toward her breasts. I reminded myself to stick to the front of her and avoid the lower back stubble, a mental caution that did nothing to interest my wanger.

In contrast to my own diffidence, I felt Carlota's animal spirits overtaking her sudden shyness, as, using both hands, she flipped the sheet down to her waist. She was in street clothes, which might have been a disappointment if I weren't thinking beyond fabrics.

She looked different, but there wasn't enough light for me to figure out what had changed, and in my state there wasn't much brain power available for puzzles.

That's when she put on a deep voice and said, "Time to get you out of here."

"We have two hours," I said, working a Barry White voice and leaning in.

"If you kiss me, I'll punch you."

I pulled back to make sense of this when she pulled off her hair and there in the near dark was Reggie.

I've had some shocks in my life, but none like this one. My mind simply could not bring this reality into focus.

Could it be that Reggie and Carlota were the same person?

"Details later," he said as he sprung from the bed. He crossed the room and peaked out the curtain. "I drugged the guard and, sure enough, he's in dreamland."

I then had the chance to check out this faux Carlota, and he did look like Newt Gingrinch in drag, which meant that he did resemble Carlota. Still, it did not seem feasible that this skinny old guy had passed for her.

"How is this possible? Where's Carlota?"

"I was the middleman. She had me set up everything about the rendezvous. Carlota thinks your conjugal is tomorrow."

"But how did you get past the guard?"

"I wore big sunglasses and in one hand I had Starbucks for him, and in the other I had this." He held up an obscene purple rubber phallus of a vibrator. "Believe me, he wasn't looking at my face."

From long habit, my first thought was about my reputation: How did it look that my date would arrive carrying such heavy equipment? But then I remembered myself and got down to the business of escaping.

Reggie quickly changed back into his usual business casual attire and stuffed the clothes into a travel bag. "I have to get these back to Carlota. I borrowed them from her closet. I wore the same outfit that was in the picture of Carlota that I gave to the clowns holding you, just to help me pass for her."

He next held up a mass of oatmeal-colored rubber hanging below a pair of sagging rubber breasts. "And this I borrowed from a high school teacher I used to date. They have teenagers wear it to get a sense of what it's like to be pregnant. Want a feel? Very realistic."

I declined, but he asked me to carry the thing as he had the travel bag in one hand and a pistol in the other. "I'll go first and pull my car around. Get ready to dive into it."

I waited for him, stroking one of the large breasts and wondering what might have been. Part of me wanted to tell Reggie thanks anyway and just leave and that I would go to the conjugal tomorrow and I would finish my work with El Papagayo and then try to figure out what was wrong with me.

But even as I rehearsed the words I would use to tell him to leave, he pulled up and I jumped into the car, and off we went, no one trying to stop us. I was headed back to my old life. Sigh.

Who Really Wanted Me Back?

WAS MY OLD LIFE there to go to? You can't go home again, and perhaps it was true you can't go to work again. In my case, there was Lunching Linda, and there was the maniac FullOfHimself divvying up my job—and no one seemed to care. Was there anyone sitting around, head in hands, asking plaintively, "How can we ever get along without good old Win-Win Cheeseley?" Certainly not my employer, my CEO, who'd been paying the kidnappers to not release me and who might just have me re-kidnapped.

Who really wanted me back? Who really cared? Only Reggie. But even Reggie thought it unwise to merely pop up at the office. He wanted me to go to spend a night at a hotel and plot my successful return. And that's just what I did.

Like a Cartridge Into a Beretta

I SIGNED IN AT A HOTEL using an alias. After all, I had an impressive list of people who'd be better off with me silenced. Reggie had a contact number for the kidnappers, and I was able to talk to El Papagayo and explain how I'd been de-kidnapped, wanting her to know that I would never have double-crossed her. I felt a strong urge to apologize, feeling that I'd let her down. She, however, was upbeat and grateful, telling me that she'd just signed "a major new account," expanding her business, and that her uncle had rewarded her with the promotion he'd been dangling. She made me a flattering and lucrative offer to serve as her consultant, and I said that I'd find a way to be her mentor and that I would study ways in which she could move into a legal business.

The next morning I went to my condo, put on my favorite suit, a blue-black Ungaro I'd found at Nordstrom's Rack, sliding into it like a cartridge into a Beretta, and put on a tie I'd bought the day before, one with tiny parrots, a tribute to the young woman who'd reminded me that I was, despite all the recent years of evidence to the contrary, useful.

I strode into my office and refused to countenance any second thoughts. The furniture was where I'd left it, and the box of tissues was still between the visitors' chairs, but none of my personal items were where I'd left them. It took me a minute to find them, carelessly tossed into a pair of boxes stuffed into a corner by the desk. However,

Linda Lunches was gone and there was no evidence left of her. Maybe it was my imagination, but I smelled pizza.

Reggie and I had come up with a simple strategy to dishearten her, and it had worked better than we'd imagined, shooting her out of the organization before we could implement Phase Two.

Here's how we did it: We'd confirmed that she was there on a "free trial" and had not negotiated a salary or benefits. Genghis, being Genghis, couldn't resist something for nothing and had taken advantage of her ego, believing that she could charm him into a lucrative salary. I'd explained to Reggie how to access my most secure employment files, including the compensation report, and he had passed that access on to her. An hour later she was gone. Once she'd seen how tiny her budget would be, including the budget for the HR Director's position, she took her freebie talents out the door.

I reestablished myself in my office and then adjusted my clothing, ready for the main event. I strode down the hall and enjoyed seeing the look on FullOfHimself's puffy self-satisfied face when he saw me standing over him in his cubicle. I didn't speak, just pointed at him and then at my office, then walked off.

He came babbling after me, telling me how great it was to see me.

I silenced him just by raising one index finger, such was the force of my new personality. "Shut the door."

I gave him more of the steely gaze, then told him the situation. "I know you were behind my kidnapping. I hope you will spend a long time in prison, showing off you tattooed ass to all your new boyfriends."

He was quick with the lies, denying everything. "It wasn't me. Let's go to the FBI right now and clear this up. I'll take a lie detector test."

The truth was I had no evidence and no way of getting any, so I wasn't eager to bring in the authorities and have to answer a lot of questions about people I did not wish to implicate. But I did have one concrete piece of evidence and that would be enough. Reggie had lifted a Coke can from FullOfHimself's desk and had his police pals run a comparison to a partial print lifted from the cartridge left on my desk, and it was solid, a match with a percentage of certainty with nine nines. I had the report with me and I slid it across my desk. He read it and figured out its meaning without questions.

His confession was nonchalant. "That's right. I left that bullet on your desk."

I gave him a *Godfather* nod, up and slow. But he didn't crumble. "I found the thing laying in the parking lot one morning and didn't know what to do with it. I didn't want to leave it out there. The guys in Security didn't know what to do with it so I came to you to ask your advice. You were off, getting a haircut or something, so I left it. Then I got busy and forgot to mention it. But I was just trying to get your advice. You keep telling me, when in doubt, ask."

I gave another slow nod, going up even more, meaning I was practically looking at the ceiling but buying some time while I figured out what to do now that my one piece of solid evidence had been explained away.

Perhaps the young creep across the desk sensed my hesitation for he leaned forward and went on the offensive. "Here is the situation we find ourselves in. I have worked my butt off for you and this company. Instead of supporting me, you have felt threatened and held me back. You wouldn't even help me get my certification for fear that I would surpass you. And now you must have heard of my applying for regional HR Executive of the Year because you come in here making wild accusations and trying to put all your problems on me. I could sue you and the company for even suggesting that I had anything to do with your kidnapping. And if you even hint that you're going to try, I'll be in my lawyer's office within the hour."

Decades of work in HR has given me the reflexes of a Labrador Retriever, that is, to look hurt and gently try to diffuse the situation by rolling over with a whimper and inviting a good belly rub. Not this time. I'd learned something about myself and my profession in my time away and I felt a hard edge rise in me and there appeared an essential truth—the Lab was once a wolf.

I startled myself by machine-gunning out this response: "We both know what scum you are and you were involved in my kidnapping. I have witnesses. You are fired. No appeal, no severance, just plain old get-your-ass-out fired. Effective yesterday. Go straight to your car and leave. I will have Security send you your things."

"You can't fire me, not without cause."

"I am firing you with the best of causes—that you are a self-centered asshole who is unworthy of working for me."

"That's bull. You have to follow the handbook. You should know that—you wrote the thing."

This brought out a fiend in me, one capable of a blasphemy of unprecedented proportions. Even now I marvel at the Winslow Cheeseley who stood and growled, oh, gods and angels of HR forgive me...

"*Fuck the employee handbook.*"

What could he say to that? Nothing. There is no higher source in our universe, and he merely sagged, defeated. I hotly repeated my assertions of his guilt and his worminess, and soon he was gone.

The Squeech of a Stepped-on Chihuahua

NEXT CAME GENGHIS. I figured he owed me. He, however, was a man who lived his life in absolute certainty that his employees owed him everything.

I strode past Eve, who looked rather shabby and gray about the eyes. She attempted to flirt with me to detain me, but I was unstoppable. As I opened his office door I saw Putin walking in beside me and I winked and said, "Watch this!"

Genghis practically spit out the mechanical pencil in his mouth. "What are you doing here?"

"My job."

I pulled up one of his visitor chairs and leaned over his desk, letting my new aura wash over him.

"I am back and have retaken my department. Linda is long gone, and I just fired Kyle." I pulled out a set of papers from the pocket inside my suit coat. "I have here the authorization to make a generous offer to a colleague of mine to become my new VP of HR. You'll like her, and you already know her husband, Senator Vilgan. While I was away I also made a list of key people it is essential we retain. A few are seriously underpaid. I am one of them. Reggie is another. The young engineer in R&D is a third. There are three others on the list. Your signature authorizes immediate salary increases. And finally, here is a list of additional expenses for Training, restoring many of the cuts of the last year, including pizza and a big red

Coke-can cooler. Sign there, and we're even."

"I don't know what those kidnappers were giving you to drink or smoke, but you are hallucinating." He pushed the papers back to me.

"Not hallucinating, preparing for my network interviews. I have invitations from all the major networks, starting with the morning programs tomorrow morning. I need to know which story to tell. The one where I sit alone with the interviewer and daub at my eyes as I tell the story of an employer who not only refused to negotiate for my release but paid the kidnappers to keep me longer while exploiting my suffering. That's the story that leads to the call for a boycott of M.I.C. products."

He let out the squeech of a stepped-on Chihuahua. "Or..." I continued before he could comment, "...there's the other story, the one I tell with you and Carlota and Reggie beside me on the couch. The one about the employee who arranged a daring rescue and how thrilled my CEO and my fiancé are to have me back and how thrilled I am that everyone is supporting me by supporting M.I.C. products." I let that concrete set, then said with gentle strength, "Your pick."

I give him credit, Genghis never forgets how to maximize profits, and he reached over and took the papers and started reading them. He started shaking his head and muttering, what I knew from long experience was the start of a whinging negotiation. I cut that off with a simple, "It's not negotiable."

"Oh, come off it. Not even the pizza? I know you threw in the pizza to have something to give up in negotiating. I know you know how to play the game."

I just gave my head one long slow shake. "This time the game is hardball, and I'm pitching a shutout or I'm getting a lot richer by suing the company that let me sit in a drop house for…"

But by then he was already signing, and I knew the old sales motto, "When they say yes, stop selling."

I stood and offered my hand, and Genghis stood and took my hand but couldn't help himself, couldn't let me think I'd won. "You know, I got the better end of that deal. The new line is our biggest hit ever."

"And I am certain that a new line of men's products will be equally successful. Maybe I'll be the spokesman for those. Meanwhile, I will have the boys in PR figure out the best way for us to work the story."

Genghis held onto the handshake, even though we'd gone well past maximum effective grip time. (I'd done seminars on The Perfect Handshake, and after eight seconds it begins to turn from compassionate to creepy.)

"How long have we been together, old friend?" he half-whispered, affecting emotion.

"Fifteen years."

"That's longer than anyone who's reported to me. Anyone. That makes you special."

That makes me nervous, not special, I thought.

"And while you're special to me, and you're the right man for the job, you're just not right for Carlota. She's an emotional mess who's never had much luck in love. So when you come along with a constant boner for her, she thinks that this is her chance to be a regular couple and have a big wedding and a baby or two. But her mother and I know it won't work for reasons I can't go into. It's just not possible."

This wonderful news felt like I'd fallen onto a feather bed and dozens of puppies were climbing over me, licking my face. I wanted to giggle, but fought back the joy.

Genghis misinterpreted my facial contortions. "I can see that you care and that this is hard, but I'm asking you as an old friend to give her up. I'm willing to double the raise for you in that requisition to try to make it up to you."

I tried to reply but was too ecstatic.

Genghis negotiated against himself as he added, "Okay, you bastard. And a twenty percent bonus."

Not wanting to grin, I merely bared my teeth and replied, "And a twenty percent increase in my department budget."

"Shit. Yes."

"But wait a minute. What about Carlota? Shouldn't she be in on this discussion?"

"I've offered her the job of heading a new European division. She wanted to take you with her, but I persuaded her to take Eve instead. I suppose she should stay to do the network interviews with you. And let me say this: She is a grown woman, and hey, if you two want to have a fling, fine. But I asked her to put off the wedding till next year. I think if she gets away from home, she'll see that it's not right for her. However, if you two are still determined a year from now, then I'll go along. It's just a year. I need you to support me on this." Then, still holding my hand, which was going numb, he said something I don't believe he has ever said before. "Please."

Sorry, Lover

WE FLEW TO NEW YORK that evening to do all the shows the next day. Genghis chose to stay home and that was fine because the cameras loved Reggie and he loved being the humble hero. Carlota looked her best, her skin flawless, and we sold a lot of product.

The FBI demanded that I spend time with them, immediately, unimpressed with the marketing imperative of the latest news cycle. So I had to say farewell to Carlota outside the NBC headquarters, the famous 30 Rock.

She leaned into me and kissed and tweaked. Her last words before jumping into the limo were, "Sorry, lover, but this way it will be even better. You'll fly over, and our first night together will be in Paris."

As for the FBI and then the local authorities, I told and retold how my captors were all of medium built with dark hair and eyes and Spanish accents and how I had no idea where I'd been held. All true.

Open or Closed?

IT'S BEEN A COUPLE OF WEEKS now that I've been back. A new salary survey came out the other day, and I was pleased to see that with my pair of raises and a bonus, that I was now up to the national average for head of HR at a medium-sized company.

My fame as a victim made me the most famous HR person in the country and I'm scheduled to be the keynote speaker at HR conferences all over the country. Can the HR Person of the Year be far behind?

Yesterday I got a call from El Papagayo, and she told me that the new immigration policies were creating a demand for the children of illegals to meet education requirements. She was starting a new business, a legal one, to help them. She asked me to help her, on the side, and I eagerly accepted.

One item still troubled me, that FullOfHimself would make good on his threats and sue the company for wrongful termination. I asked Reggie to come to my office to talk about that.

"I went to visit Kyle yesterday," he told me solemnly. "I told him we had eye witnesses that had seen him at the meeting with the kidnappers."

"True, but you know we can't get them to testify."

"I know, and you know. He doesn't know. And then I told him to think back to that meeting and whether he'd taken his cellphone along. I reminded him that the police can get the records of where he was that day, even when he wasn't using the phone."

"Is that true?"

"Sure, if he took the phone with him, and I could see in his weaselly eyes that he had. And that's when his pretensions went poof. All he had left was trying to act all above-it-all. He waved me off and declared that he, was 'putting all that behind me' and 'only looking forward now.' So..." Reggie did a quick four beats using my desktop for a drum, "...he caved, he's gone, and we never have to worry about him again."

"That's great. *You've* been great. Just great."

"I know."

He stood to leave. "And the raise was nice, but it has me worried."

"Don't worry. It's in the system. It's solid."

"It's not that. It's that I used to be a bargain for this company, and with the raise, I'm not. They could hire someone younger for less money. And I heard a rumor this morning about new layoffs."

"Not true." Was it? I hadn't seen Genghis in a couple days. "But don't worry. There's no way that they're getting rid of you. I would never allow that to happen."

"Hey, you're not a bargain anymore, either. Who says you'll be here to not allow it?"

He had a point, but I was worry-weary and couldn't think about it. Wanting to change the subject, I played at being wistful and sighed, "I keep thinking how sweet you looked in bed at the hotel."

"I already gave back the pregnancy suit, but I could see if you could borrow it." He winked and turned to go. He paused as he stepped through the doorway. "You want this open or closed."

"Thanks for asking. Closed."

With a satisfying chlunk, the door latched. My door.

To The Reader

This is my first novel. I'm a rookie again, at my age. Imagine that.

I welcome your thoughts and your assistance.

First, if you found mistakes, please let me know, and I'll correct them for the next printing. If you found laughs or wisdom or any other form of entertainment, please let me know at dale@dauten.com... and please tell your friends, coworkers and, most of all, tell your HR person.

If you'd like to be included in a mailing list about future books and articles, please sign up at Dauten.com

Acknowledgements

One of the joys of writing this book was getting to have conversations about life and work with a number of wise and clever people. Among them were two people in HR who were willing to help me understand their professional lives, Azure Spanier and Gary Starzmann. (I am pleased to report that their work lives seem much more agreeable than those of the HR staff at Mundane Industries.)

I was also grateful to my old colleague, Tony Lesce, for his help in understanding bullets, cartridges, and rifles.

As for the writing itself, I am grateful for the advice and guidance of three talented friends: Mark Nykanen, Janet Traylor and Jim Fickess.

I am also indebted to Chris Jones and Diane Buhl for their editing and to Chris Molé for her design work.

As always, my love to Jeri, Diane, Sandy, Hilary, Trevor, Joel, David, Dana and Ava.

And, finally, I acknowledge my indebtedness to the great P.G. Wodehouse. A signed photo of "Plum" watched over me as I wrote this book. If you know his work, then I hope you found yourself smiling at my nods to Bertie and Jeeves.

Made in the USA
Charleston, SC
30 December 2013